CUTHBERT
A Fair Cop in the Valley

#9

by

Patrick Barrett

A Wild Wolf Publication

Published by Wild Wolf Publishing in 2016
Copyright © 2016 Patrick Barrett

First print

All characters appearing in this work are fictitious. Any resemblance to real persons, living or dead, is purely coincidental.

ISBN: 978-1-907954-58-0
Also available as an e-book

www.wildwolfpublishing.com

Chapter One

Jasper settled back in the branches of the tree and scanned the Valley for intruders. He smiled to himself; this was his excuse to escape the demands of running the Valley mafia and pretend that he alone could keep everyone safe.

He stretched lazily and peered towards the entrance of the Valley. He had been disappointed with this tree at first because he didn't have a clear view, but the odd thing was that after he had dozed off for a while the view had been perfect when he woke up. "That's all this Valley needs," he sniggered, "moving trees."

Jasper tore a corner off his sandwich and tossed it to the crow who was keeping watch from a higher branch. The crow caught the bread expertly but stayed tensed and ready for flight, he *knew* that the tree had moved.

Inside the tree, Ronald peered through a knot-hole at the winding approach road. After a successful career as a mercenary, he had begun to stock up on sniper hide replica trees in case his fake obituaries caused him real problems. He had similar trees scattered about the Valley, but he had forgotten where most of them were and this resulted in him wandering about tapping random trunks and convincing the Captain that a rare Siberian woodpecker was in residence.

Jasper tried to estimate the time, when something caught his eye by assessing the length of various shadows before giving up and looking at his watch instead. You didn't get many blue flashing lights in the Valley except when, "Blooming heck," he exclaimed.

"What?" Ronald asked.

"There," said Jasper pointing, apparently for the benefit of a tree.

Jasper looked at the crow and the crow shrugged in return as the tree began to make its escape before bumping into another fake tree and starting an avalanche of papier-mâché' timber rolling downhill. Now, the Valley mafia had branches everywhere and Jasper wasn't sure which posed the biggest danger, the copse or the cops.

Chapter Two

Henry and Margery were standing outside The Mandrake Arms when the procession of police cars entered the main street and even though they had been relatively innocent for years, their mental filing systems went into overdrive at the sight and they held hands in a mutual defence pact.

As several residents gathered, a senior figure began to wait for Constable Beeching to extricate himself from his car, but upon seeing the performance taking place, he addressed the crowd instead. Ladies and gentlemen," he began. "There is no need for alarm. In response to the raging crime-wave taking place in the Valley, we have decided to become a permanent presence here." He waited gamely for a round of applause, but when he met a wall of puzzled looks, he continued. "Constable Beeching has been fighting this tide alone and his reports can no longer be ignored."

He turned to involve a different section of the crowd and disappeared in a cloud of 'peach-blossom' powder from Mrs Biggle's compact and was reduced to coughing and spluttering helplessly.

Constable Beeching was soon at his side to fill in the details. "Mrs Biggle here had her post office stolen sir, there's the hole right there."

Beeching's superior officer wiped his eyes and surveyed the site. "Perfect," he said, "That's where we will build our new high-tech police station."

The crowd swayed slightly as if the Valley had moved under their feet.

* * *

4

Cuthbert poured the tea as everyone tried to catch up. "What crime wave?" asked Henry, looking suspiciously at the pot plant in the corner, but Jasper just waved a frond listlessly.

Ronald contributed, "It's that constable colossus and his make-believe reports, they think the mafia operates here now."

"They do," said Cuthbert.

"Not this bunch of juvenile delinquents," sneered Ronald, "The really dangerous ones." But even as he spoke, he began to realise just how many pot plants Cuthbert suddenly had and wisely shut up.

The Captain was looking distracted and he suddenly leant forward and tapped Ronald on the chest making a hollow clunk. "Are you wearing a papier-mâché' bullet proof vest?" he asked, "You'll scare that Siberian woodpecker away playing tricks like that."

Ronald glared. Most of his disguise had smashed as he rolled downhill, but he was still encased in part of the trunk and his arms were waving feebly, like a cartoon T-rex.

Chapter Three

Marvin Middlewick had never had an office full of policemen before. Of course, constable Beeching would have achieved that alone, so they made him stay outside.

The senior officer had already apologised to Marvin when he saw the 'C.L.O.S.E.D' sign on his desk and had received the news that Marvin was the 'Council Liaison Officer Specialising in Excavations and Digging' and he was now addressing Marvin. "I am Chief Inspector Peebles and to combat the incessant crime wave in the Valley, we intend to build the most advanced police station in the country on the site of the old post office."

Marvin suddenly paid attention. "Can you do that, do you own the land, is it legal?"

The officer was astonished. "Of course it's legal, we're the police."

The two men stared at each other as the implications of a possible power struggle became obvious, but the Chief Inspector ploughed on. "We will need surveyors to map the site and experts to examine the foundations. Can you provide those for us?"

Marvin nodded mutely, surveyors, foundation investigators, drains inspectors, striped tents and vans. It sounded more like an invasion and nothing good ever came from invading the Valley.

* * *

The Valley mafia could see this being a real problem, but Jasper had long ago learnt the knack of turning problems into profits. Take tonight for instance, they had called an emergency meeting of all the nearby valleys in one of the big tunnel rooms, but after converting it with all the flashing lights they had stolen from the police cars, they were charging for a disco instead.

* * *

Meanwhile, another meeting was taking place in the theatre where all the locals sat expectantly as Chief Inspector Peebles and his team shuffled papers on tables and waited for another irritating shuffling to stop in the audience.

Eventually, two large constables lifted Percy and jammed the front legs of his chair into his wellies and the meeting began.

After outlining the facts again and explaining that this 'Centre of policing excellence' would bring peace and security to this secluded Valley; the officer sat down and prepared for questions.

Constable Beeching sat behind him and every time someone spoke, he whispered in his superior's ear. It reminded Henry of Ancient Rome where a slave stood behind Caesar during a processional triumph whispering "You are only mortal" in his ear, to try to keep his ego at bay.

The questions started with Avril. "Chief Inspector, I am the local reporter for The Triple Echo and I have no knowledge of any crime wave. Could you clarify this please?"

The officer leant to one side as Constable Beeching whispered, "This one is the reporter from The Triple Echo sir and she doesn't know about any crime wave."

Chief Inspector Peebles smiled a thin smile before he asked, "Did you park your car outside madam? Is it still there? Did you lock your office when you left madam? Is it still there? This is the thing about crime, it takes a professional to recognise it and when the general public notices it, it's too late and everything's gone."

Avril sat down heavily.

Geraldine leapt to her feet to announce, "I am the museum curator and I would like your assurance that the priceless treasures contained inside, will have your top priority."

The officer leant sideways again as constable Beeching whispered "This is the museum curator sir and she wants to know if you will respect her topiary."

The officer paused for a moment before asking, "Ancient treasures eh, are they from all around the world madam?"

Geraldine beamed. "Oh yes, Egypt, Persia, Assyria and even Rome itself."

The officer rubbed his chin, "Fascinating, absolutely fascinating. It must be difficult to keep on top of filing all those receipts and removal permissions and antiquity travel permits my dear, we will definitely be paying you a visit."

Geraldine sat down heavily.

Henry stood and used his best placatory ex-news reader tones to address the stage. "Surely, we can accept that most of these acts have been simple youthful exuberance, it's hardly a crime wave now is it?"

Constable Beeching whispered, "Ha, now the alibi's start, this one's clever, I've never arrested him."

"Henry Chisholm, is it? Your reputation goes before you, but your paperwork shows that your passport often doesn't match the dates you were in the war zones and yet your brother Ronald was definitely there, usually just before you. Interesting isn't it?"

Henry sat down heavily.

It was obvious now to anyone with a brain, that this was a very dangerous man to deal with, so the next question came as a surprise to everyone.

"So, what do you do all day, count the feathers?" asked Percy.

"What?" spluttered the officer desperately needing a whisper from constable Beeching?

When you inspect chiefs," insisted Percy, "Do you fine them if there's a feather missing?"

"Slippery one this one," whispered Beeching "claims to be a gardener, had him in my cells many times."

"Well, why is he here now then?" hissed the Chief Inspector furiously.

Beeching shrugged, "He kept picking the locks, so I took the cell doors off to stop him."

The Inspector gaped.

The Captain stood up next, "I'm not sure I like your tone, you know officer. You sound as if you'll be making this a police state."

"The state it's in, anything would be an improvement," snapped the policeman, quickly gathering his papers and causing his assistants to flap about around him as he headed for the exit.

Stopping and turning in the doorway, he left them with one last thought, "The only people who need to fear the police are those who have committed a crime, or are contemplating committing a crime, or may someday commit a crime to test the theory that crime pays. Believe you, my people, crime does not pay, it is merely the wages of sin." And he stormed out with an evangelical flounce.

The audience of residents were gasping and reliving the highlights of the meeting as they accepted cups of tea from Elspeth's ever-present tea urn and they gradually frowned at a persistent interruption of bumps and bangs and muttered curses.

Eventually, they all formed a circle and watched as Percy repeatedly tried to stand up from the chair he was sitting on, whilst the front legs were down his wellies and gravity was having a rare day of levity at his expense.

Chapter Four

No-one asked Percy how he had eventually freed himself when he joined the gathering at Cuthbert's kitchen table, but if he had been a cartoon, there would have been a black cloud over his head.

The Captain was saying, "Can't say I liked that chap at all, he's going to be trouble."

Henry nodded in agreement and Ronald crept in from a back room somewhere with slightly less of a mock tree around him than there had been earlier, but more cuts and scratches than anyone remembered.

Henry watched Cuthbert bustling about with the kettle and he frowned at a sudden thought, "Where were you Cuthbert?"

All eyes turned to Cuthbert causing him to put the kettle down so that more of his 'fight or flight' instincts would be directed to his legs should he need it and his intellectual prowess retorted with "pardon?"

Henry sighed, "You weren't at the meeting and none of this seems to bother you at all."

"Oh that," said Cuthbert on more solid ground now that he thought that he might actually have some idea of what the topic was. "I've heard it all before, no-one listened to me, but they ended up scrapping the whole idea."

Everyone sat up straight, "You've beaten this plan before?" asked Henry. "That's wonderful, how did you do it and how can we do it again?"

Cuthbert sat proudly at the head of the table and began to explain that the old tunnels wouldn't take the weight and the new tunnels would have to be blasted through the hills to reach the Valley and that the big water tank would block his view and the rails would go straight through the cemetery and everyone took the bus anyway.

His audience gaped until Ronald stabbed himself with a fork to orientate his thoughts and shouted "Police station you nitwit, not Train station."

Percy hadn't even heard the exchange; he was fumbling about under the table trying to get a broken chair leg out of his welly.

* * *

The ladies were gathered in the Mandrake Arms and the atmosphere was quite revolutionary. There was talk of barricading Mrs Biggle's crater with furniture and repelling all invaders, this was met with enthusiastic approval until Elspeth asked "Whose furniture?"

The conversation stalled until someone said, "Well obviously not mine, it's all top quality is mine."

Elspeth retorted with, "Well mine has been collected from all over the world during our travels."

Arkle sneered, "I've seen that foreign stuff; takes hours to build and goes flat again as soon as I sit on it."

Margery looked at Geraldine who spluttered, "Not mine, it all belongs to the museum and it's got labels on."

Avril came in next with, "I only have the office furniture and it's bolted down in case Cuthbert comes in and I throw it at him."

Mrs Biggle sighed pathetically and Margery patted her hand as they all silently acknowledged that all hers had been blown to smithereens.

Margery sensed all eyes upon her and she snapped, "Well, if I used mine, you lot would all be sat on the floor wouldn't you?"

Mrs Biggle sighed again, "So, no barricades with handsome young men shouting revolutionary slogans then?"

Geraldine laughed "We're having enough trouble finding furniture, where would we find handsome young men?"

The conversation slowly died as thoughts became daydreams floating above their heads only to burst when they hit the ceiling of reality.

Chapter Five

The drains inspector was pacing up and down before his team and trying to reassure them. "This is a top security operation men," he said "The police will be everywhere and Marvin has promised us new tools and a new tent to put in the van we had stolen last Wednesday."

'One-lung Louie' had spotted the flaw in that statement, but all anyone heard was "Hurr-hurr," because he was excited.

'Swivelling Simon' wasn't keen on too much contact with the police because sometimes his replacement glass eyes came from a contact at the waxworks and Buster always got confused when the one on traffic duty started waving his arms at him.

The drains inspector suddenly remembered an inspirational sentence he had heard somewhere and fixed each of his team with a determined look "Remember men, life may be a ball but we didn't come here to dance."

* * *

Ronald had insisted upon meeting on the hillside because his military instincts warned him not to be caught in a building.

Henry and the Captain watched patiently as Ronald constructed a hide from his broken mock trees and made sure he wasn't silhouetted against the skyline before convening today's event.

"This chap is going to be trouble. PC Plonker has created such a list of fake crimes to stay in a job that no-one will question the need for a new police station."

The Captain shrugged, "Dashed hard to take on the whole police force though chaps, but will it really bother us?"

Ronald was appalled, "Speed cameras, tax discs, licenses, and permits; even Whistle will need a fishing license for the dry reservoir."

Henry shrugged, "We do cut the odd corner as publicans and it's always nice to buy some cheap pasties from the zoo in the next valley."

Both Ronald and the Captain made a mental note to stick to crisps in future.

"Train Station," giggled Percy "Don't you ever listen to anything Cuthbert?"

Cuthbert glared, "I seem to spend an awful lot of time listening to *you* mate, perhaps that's where I developed selective deafness."

Chapter Six

Avril sat in her office and stared at Chief Inspector Peebles. She had to admit that he looked rather dashing in his uniform with all the decorative braid and she felt herself blushing slightly as he spoke.

"Now Avril, may I call you Avril?"

He was rewarded by a nod so he continued. "I always make a point of getting the press on-side, so that we can share information and head off any difficulties. You are probably the most qualified woman in the Valley and I need someone I can trust and respect."

Avril gaped; here was someone who understood, someone who could see how her career had become bogged down in this backwater. "How can I help?" she purred.

Peebles smiled, "Let's start with the Valley mafia shall we?"

Avril began to speak, ignoring the warning bells in her head and the pot plant in the corner, which hadn't been there yesterday.

* * *

Percy was sat outside on the horse trough when Chief Inspector Peebles left Avril's office and the two eyed each other warily. Pc Beeching had warned his boss about this master criminal and master of disguise, but it seemed to the Inspector that any competent copper with a nose for trouble would simply follow the smell from Percy's wellies.

The officer approached Percy and asked "Had a chequered career then have you lad, been a bit of a knave have we?"

This confused Percy, who wasn't sure whether they were discussing chess or cards, so he headed for more familiar territory. "One of my ancestors was with you lot, you know" he said. "Head of the firearms division and involved in all the major shoot-outs."

The Chief Inspector paused. He was always prepared to listen to background information for his files. It was amazing what people gave away voluntarily, "You don't say? Tell me more." He hissed.

Percy shuffled to get comfortable, "Well," he began, "he was called out by a foot patrol who heard gunfire from a city centre street and he immediately cordoned off the street and cancelled the Queen's visit. All the traffic was re-routed and everybody was evacuated until only my relative and a small team were left. He ordered everyone to stay where they were and insisted on going in alone because he was single and apparently it sounded like 'The Saint Valentine's Day Massacre' in there."

The Chief Inspector gasped "That must have won him a medal at least."

Percy waved dismissively, "Unknown to him, the Fire Brigade was at the back of the premises and they were preparing to enter as well."

"What happened, what happened?" gasped the officer.

"Well," said Percy as his shoulders slumped, "Everything happened at once, my relative braced himself against all the bangs and entered the balloon shop from the front, just as the Fire Brigade went in the back and rescued the hedgehog."

The officer's brain took its time analysing whether it was suffering an embolism or not, and by the time it gave the all-clear, Percy was gone.

* * *

The bar of The Mandrake Arms was a strange place to be at the moment. The men were instinctively quiet as Margery clattered out her displeasure in a Morse code of bumps and bangs and clonks and clanks as glasses were rearranged for no reason whatsoever.

As her husband, it was really Henry's responsibility to ask what was wrong, but he was ignoring all the raised eyebrows and nods in her direction and trying to think of an excuse to go for a walk.

Eventually, Elspeth managed to sigh with an intensity which attracted everyone's attention and asked "What's wrong dear?"

Margery paused before replying, "Wrong?" (Crash) "Wrong?" (Bang) "That cow who runs the pub in the next valley has just come back from a cruise, that's what's wrong. When is the last time I had a holiday, or went on a cruise?"

This remark was directed at Henry with an accompanying glare. Henry waited silently for salvation, it soon came and oddly enough it was from Elspeth.

"There's a reason for everything dear," she said, "I bet I know who was running the cruise."

Margery had calmed down slightly and was breathing quite normally when she asked, "Who would that be then dear?"

Elspeth smiled, "Why Noah of course, he needed another mad-cow to make a pair."

Chapter Seven

Cecil Carruthers stood looking at the crater; his assistant Winston jiggled about beside him, firmly plugged into a headset and playing air-guitar with the striped surveying pole. Cecil sighed, the history of his profession filled his mind, the civil engineering expertise of the world was at his fingertips and they had asked him to fill a hole. Not just any hole of course, a hole in the Valley where anything could happen, vans disappeared, holes disappeared and even people disappeared. Everything disappeared, except Cecil's headache, could things get any worse?

"Watcha doin'?" asked Percy; standing behind them.

Chief Inspector Peebles looked around Constable Beeching's police station in an assessment of whether it could be his temporary headquarters; the assessment didn't take long as there was no furniture and only one cell had a door.

"What on earth happened here, Constable?" he asked.

Beeching thought he was being asked to account for every fast-food stain and gravy smear, but his superior was suddenly being very specific.

"Where is the cell door?" he demanded.

Beeching was proud of this one, so he puffed out his chest and replied, "I sold it, to stop the notorious burglar Percy Plumm from picking the lock sir, my escape ratio halved instantly." He quivered to attention; well, his body quivered and he may well have been at attention somewhere in there.

"Where is the door now Constable?" hissed the Chief Inspector.

"At the end of the tunnel, sir," was the immediate reply.

"What tunnel?" asked his boss.

"The one leading to the concrete lake, sir" said Beeching confidently.

"Concrete lake?" spluttered his questioner, "Why do you have a concrete lake man?"

Beeching began to explain that Aunt Liza (shudder) had poured concrete down the tunnels to stop the Valley folk 'sneaking about,' then she had sealed the end up to stop the Valley folk sabotaging her theatre project after they had fired coconut bombs at it, but because all the tunnels sloped downwards, the concrete ran into the lake and set solid.

The Chief Inspector shook his head and looked around, "Where do you keep your files?" he asked.

Constable Beeching rummaged in his top pocket and proudly produced a manicure set.

"Not those, you dimwit; the crime records, the misdemeanour files, the wanted posters," screeched his exasperated superior.

Beeching slumped dramatically (Percy would have been proud of him.)

"Lost in the fire sir," he said dejectedly.

"Fire, what fire?" demanded a man barely holding on to reason.

"Oh, it was during the 'Inter-Valley Wars' sir, besieged in here I was sir, I has to burn them to send smoke signals for reinforcements."

The Chief Inspector dragged his feet as he headed for the door, he was being told by obscure parts of his brain that no good would come of this, but he had been allocated the funds for the project and there was no such thing as a form for refunding public money.

Just as he crossed the threshold, he looked back at Beeching "Did you say there's a theatre?" he asked.

Chapter Eight

A sense of lethargy had settled inside Cuthbert's kitchen, either that or the cooking range had finally marshalled all its carbon monoxide and breathed it over the occupants. The knocking at the door sounded official, it was always hard to tell how it sounded *official*, but compared with the door being flat on the floor SAS style at one extreme and the timorous tapping of a misplaced corpse at the other, this one came in-between.

Percy dragged himself to his feet and peered through a crack in the door before fleeing into another room.

Henry sighed and followed suit, but after a glance through the crack, he headed for a secret passage, followed by the Captain who knew a lost cause when he saw it.

Ronald crept ninja-style and peered between the smudges and grim of the window; it was enough and he too was off.

Cuthbert waited for the second bout of knocking and opened the door, letting this simple action determine his fate.

Chief Inspector Peebles pushed past and took in the scene, "So this is where the master producer practices his scene setting eh? Is this some scruffy old kitchen from Tudor times? Well done." Then he noticed the half empty steaming cups "Ahh, the deserted galley of The Marie Celeste eh? Brilliant, it's very authentic."

Cuthbert actually felt quite relaxed with this chap, he seemed happy to talk away to himself and didn't need any answers and even Percy came back in and joined them at the table.

Cuthbert even thought that he may be able to wander off to bed in a minute and leave them both to it but then he groaned inwardly as the questions began. Cuthbert found himself explaining how William Shakespeare was rumoured to have taught the family at Mandrake Hall long before it had burnt down and written his first plays in the Valley, but he had left them behind because they were critical of Queen Elizabeth and some of them were still hidden amongst the tunnels and secret passages. This fact was commemorated every year by a terrible local production of one of his plays.

The policeman leant forward and exclaimed, "Do you realise that it's Shakespeare's birthday today?"

Cuthbert assumed the expression which was often mistaken by strangers for evidence that he was considering his reply. Actually, he was panicking because he didn't have a clue.

Fortunately, Percy came to the rescue with, "It would have been earlier, but all that "to be or not to be" nonsense in the womb held him up."

The Chief Inspector was appalled. "I am a huge fan of the Bard and I was prepared to take part in one of your plays, Cuthbert, but now I see that I may have to take over. Good day to you both." He flounced out.

Cuthbert sighed, just when he thought everyone had forgotten that he was the custodian of the biggest carnival of errors since Helen of Troy announced, "I know, let's launch a thousand ships and hold a regatta" someone wanted to resurrect the annual play.

To bring Cuthbert out of his reverie, Percy banged a fresh cup of tea in front of him and said, "That was close, mate; he almost thought you were the real thing."

Chapter Nine

Avril was excited, the visit from the Chief Inspector had inspired her; she could gain access to privileged information and scoop all the other newspapers. Her moment had come she thought, as she gazed at the two pot plants on the far wall. That's odd, she thought, do they really breed that fast? She must ask Percy.

Leaves rustled behind her and a voice whispered "We hear you've been talking."

Avril fainted.

* * *

The assemblage around Cuthbert's kitchen table had mixed feelings about both the Chief Inspector and performing a new play. Basically, they agreed that someone sensible should take over the production, but how would the Valley function when the enemy of the people was in constant attendance?

This comment side-tracked things nicely as both Percy and Ronald objected to being enemies of the people whilst at the same time hoping for the notoriety.

Cuthbert wasn't sure whether he had been promoted or demoted and Henry and the Captain knew that it couldn't possibly refer to them.

Silence followed as they stared into the scrying pools of Cuthbert's tea-cups. Something must have shown up in the sediment because Henry suddenly asked, "Which play did he have in mind Cuthbert?"

Cuthbert shrugged, "No idea, he went off muttering about seeing a merchant of Venice."

"Perhaps he's buying some scenery" suggested Ronald.

"What's wrong with ours?" demanded an affronted Cuthbert.

The Captain scoffed, "Cuthbert, we're still using the backdrop of a wooded scene with a stag on it and it wasn't even designed for Macbeth."

Ronald smirked, "We could paint over its antlers and say it was a dog named Tempest."

Henry waited for the sniggers to die down and asked Cuthbert "Did you give him a list of the plays we've already done?"

Cuthbert returned Henry's gaze with a look that said "You've bid one question I can't answer so I'll raise you one reply you can't hear."

Henry waited a polite amount of time before asking "Do you have a list of the ones we've done Cuthbert?"

All eyes flicked from one adversary to the other as if it was a tennis match where only one player had a racket.

Henry tried another tack "Cuthbert, do you have a list of *anything* Shakespeare wrote?"

Percy simply could not keep out of this so he chimed in with, "Knows them all by heart, he does Henry, only last night he said he wanted to do the one where some chap shouts 'Julius, seize her.'"

Ronald joined in with, "So that's the name of the dog on the island then."

Once more, Cuthbert was alone in a gale of laughter and derision which somehow seemed to radiate out from him, if only he could figure out how he caused it, he could stop doing it, but he suspected that it would involve a complete character change.

* * *

Avril had been revived by a pot plant solicitously waving a frond in her face to give her some fresh air and then she had signed some sort of scrawled contract which apparently committed her to 'Complete secrecy with regards to the Valley Mafia and its doings or intentions on pain of several Indian burns and black finger nails.' Actually, she didn't mind the thought of them painting her nails, but she would rather pick her own colour. She sighed; her office seemed rather bare without the pot plants.

* * *

Constable Beeching was trying to be secretly pleased with his progress so far. He had rocketed to the top of the crime fighting statistics and even managed to have a police station built on the main

22

street; perhaps they would name it after him after they left him in peace in his own secluded out-station. He leant back in his patrol car set for a contented forty winks, but failed to see the mafia slithering towards him underneath the height of his door mirrors.

* * *

Margery was also trying to weigh up the pro's and cons of the new police station. On the one hand it meant extra customers and these new ones might actually buy more than one drink unlike her present crop. But, on the other hand it may just clip the mafia's wings. Jasper was more than a match for the lot of them, but they only had to realise that school days didn't seem to apply in the Valley and there could soon be another building in the Valley with even tougher bars then the police station.

Chapter Ten

The road gang were also looking into the crater, but at a discreet distance from the surveyor and his assistant; this was to preserve the status quo, or that's what they assumed that Winston was jigging about to.

"Did you bring the sandwiches Louie?" asked the drains inspector.

"Yes boss," answered Louie promptly.

"Did someone bring the thermos?" he asked next.

"Yes boss," affirmed Simon swivelling one eye as a shrub moved nearby.

"Everything's in the van boss," said Buster impatiently.

"Where's the van?" asked the drains inspector.

* * *

Constable Beeching leapt into action when his radio squawked "Stolen van, all units in the Valley pursue and apprehend unknown suspects."

Seeing as there was only one road into or out of the Valley, the constable would be hard-pressed to avoid being involved in this one, but his patrol car seemed to have ideas of its own. The engine roared, but the scenery around him didn't seem to move at all and he had a clear view of it as well with all the doors missing.

* * *

Cuthbert was feeling under pressure; if this Chief Inspector really knew a lot about Shakespeare and his plays, he would soon decide that Cuthbert had been bluffing all these years. The truth was that Cuthbert used any old scrap of parchment he found in the secret tunnels or compartments and claimed it as a lost play and if there was a bit missing, he would add another piece of paper from somewhere else to fill it out. That's why Henry had been puzzled when the merchant of Venice had tried to claim tax relief on his new tractor.

Fortunately, like all clubs and associations, the majority of members wanted someone else to do all the work and make all the decisions so that they could drink sherry once a week and criticise the chap who did all the work and made all the decisions.

Cuthbert wandered through the house trying to remember where all the secret cupboards were; sometimes it could be really irritating when the whole house was a filing system.

* * *

Percy had entered the bar in the Mandrake Arms just as Margery had asked Ronald to pass some glasses down from a high shelf and he had stood back to let the Captain reach up there. This was a major embarrassment for the man who had tamed wild animals and subdued whole countries, but no-one mentioned it until Percy spoke.

"Don't worry about being short Ronnie, one of my ancestors solved the problem years ago but we decided that the best things come in small packages and we never bothered with it."

Ronald's expressions changed from furious to curious, but suspecting something spurious, but he just had to ask "What do you mean solved it?"

Percy shuffled and explained "Well, one of the women in my family was so badly teased, she was known as Tinkerbell Plumm and she tried everything to help her grow: ointments, liniments, lotions, potions and stretching. Of course, with most of her relatives being gardeners, she realised that plants need fresh air and sun before they will grow, so she took her bed outside and slept out there to catch the early morning rays. Well, of course her mother was worried about her getting cold, so as soon as Tinkerbell was asleep, her mum would wrap her hands and feet in anything woollen we could spare."

His audience was mesmerised and Ronald was taking secret notes under the table.

"What happened, what happened?" insisted Margery.

Percy sat forward, his excitement was infectious and they all leant in as well. "Well, she woke up one morning to find woollen socks on her hands; she was thrilled. It meant that she had grown at least two feet during the night."

In one of those moments when the universe takes over and erases events which are too big to comprehend, Percy left the bar and everyone forgot that he had been there.

* * *

Marvin Middlewick heard a tap on his office window; this could mean only one thing, the road gang was outside because they weren't allowed inside, and as usual, it also meant trouble which was actually two things.

Marvin wondered how his day could always complicate itself. He sighed, stood and opened the window just enough to allow sound to enter, but to filter the smell of drains and prepared himself to hear how his men had been almost massacred by the marauding tribes of the Valley.

* * *

Jasper was having a good day, he had been in the next valley where he had sold a van full of equipment to the council, a striped tent to the church for the village fete, four wheels to the local garage and four car doors to different repair yards. He thought he might have trouble off-loading car doors emblazoned with the word 'Police,' but two of them reading 'Pol' were to customise a girl-racers car and the other two marked 'Ice' were being fitted to an ice-cream van, so it all worked out quite well. Now, he was sat by the roadside eating sandwiches and pouring a nice hot drink from his thermos.

* * *

Cuthbert was wracking his brains to remember all the plays they had performed over the years. He remembered the one where they all dressed in tights and carried swords, or was that the other one? He carried on looking.

* * *

Henry, the Captain and Ronald were still in the bar and although they had the feeling that something had happened recently they simply couldn't recall it.

Margery was cleaning glasses and she had the distinct feeling that if she spotted Percy, it would all come back to her.

* * *

Constable Beeching was now in a quandary. He had abandoned his patrol car which had magically shed all its wheels and doors and he was rolling down yet another hill because his shape simply did not agree with gravity when it came to negotiating slopes. He looked as if he had been trampled by a herd of elephants. An idea for his crime report began to form.

* * *

The conversation in the bar was back on familiar territory as the Captain and Ronald tried to outdo each other with war stories and tales of faraway lands and lost civilisations.

The Captain sighed, "It was the deserts I loved you know, living in tents with the Bedouins and the Berbers, some of the finest goatherds and hairdressers in the whole continent."

Ronald sneered, "Sounds like a bunch of Berber barbers getting on each others goats to me."

"Berber barber?" asked Margery mischievously, "did he have a wife named Barbara?"

The Captain was aghast, "Did you know them?" he asked.

Ronald took over by claiming to have been at death's door so many times that he would take a screwdriver next time and steal the knocker.

The Captain retorted by pointing out that his exploits had resulted in death pinning a note to his door saying 'round the back, use the side gate.'

Margery paused from cleaning another glass and said wearily, "All these experiences you men claim to have had, have you learned anything at all?"

The Captain puffed out his chest, "Oh yes my dear; I wear boots for the chemists, sandals when I'm preaching to Elspeth and trainers when I teach a dog to sit. Who says men can't think on their feet?"

Margery waited for the masculine laughter to stop before pointing out, "Well, we don't have a chemist, Elspeth takes absolutely no notice of you whatsoever and you just try that on blind Pugh mate."

The Captain slumped.

Chapter Eleven

Percy had been out hunting, not the kind where you need a gun or a bow or have to do anything exerting. He was truffle-hunting; one of his old gardening magazines had explained that these wild fungi fetched big money in the posh restaurants in the West End. He didn't know where the West End was or how far you went west before you found the end, but that was mere detail compared to the fact that he wasn't sure what a truffle looked like.

After hours of trudging about hoping to find something with a garden centre label still attached to it, he ended up at the empty reservoir where 'Whistle' was patiently trying to entice the non-existent fish onto his un-baited hook.

Percy had only just noticed this anomaly and when he pointed it out, Whistle's hand disappeared into his hood where Percy assumed that he was tapping the side of his nose. "Fisherman's secret Percy," he said "These fish are particularly cunning, that's why I can't catch any as it is, so if I put any bait on the hook, it would really give the game away and they would avoid me."

Percy was impressed; this was his kind of logic.

* * *

Cuthbert was scratching his head now, all the plays they had done involved men in tights and carrying swords, so he couldn't tell one from another. A faint stirring began which sometimes signalled the beginning of his thought process or could have been caused by all that scratching.

When the likes of Henry, Ronald and the Captain had moved into the Valley, they had been looking for manuscripts written by the Bard when he taught at Mandrake Hall.

There had been forgotten documents turning up in secret panels behind Cuthbert's wainscoting for years; Cuthbert began tapping the walls knowing full well that if someone tapped back, it would probably be Margery coming the other way, *probably*.

* * *

The road gang stood around expectantly. The works department were all out of striped tents and they had thoughtfully provided a bouncy castle for the team to shelter in, but when Buster lit the stove for a cuppa, the whole thing exploded causing Mrs Biggle to run down the street blowing powder from her compact and shouting that the army had fired another shell and destroyed the new police station.

The drains inspector sighed as his men rolled up the remains of the castle until it looked like a giant chrysalis and nodded wearily to the mafia who would have taken it from the back of the van anyway. Lord only knew what they wanted it for, probably best not to ask.

* * *

Henry, Ronald and the Captain had convened in Cuthbert's kitchen, interrupting his search for yet another lost play which may be or may not be in Cuthbert's walls. Hmm, he thought 'may be or not to be eh?' perhaps he could write his own play.

Percy joined them at the table weary from walking fruitlessly and fungus-ly for miles.

"How did the trifle hunt go Percy?" asked Cuthbert with mock gravitas.

Percy's eyes widened before he exploded, "Trifle, *trifle*? You let me walk all that way without telling me that, I would have spotted one of those from miles away," and he stormed out slamming the door behind him.

Breaking the following silence, Henry muttered "Wait for it, wait for it."

They all pretended not to notice as realisation dawned and Percy slinked back in and took a seat.

Cuthbert had shared his concerns about the Chief Inspector being an expert on Shakespeare and everyone around the table expressed false shock and horror that there might be some slight faults within Cuthbert's productions. Cuthbert was reassured by all this and he decided to ask for help. "Does anyone remember the name of that play we did where everyone wore tights and carried swords?"

After a pause, Henry suggested "Most of them?" and Cuthbert duly wrote it down.

30

The Captain seemed to have elected himself as amusement officer for the day and he regaled them with a tale of his trip to a supermarket in the next valley where he met a man with one arm carrying a light bulb.

When the Captain asked what he was doing, the man replied "I'm going to change this light bulb."

The Captain was stunned, "You can't change a light bulb with one arm," he challenged. "Yes I can, I've got the receipt" said the man walking away.

This of course let Percy in with, "Did I tell you that one of my ancestors was one of the first electricians?"

"Another bright spark, was he?" Ronald sneered.

Percy ignored him and explained that his relative had been at the cutting edge of the technology. He had helped to develop a generator which supplied electricity when a handle was turned; the faster it turned the more voltage it produced, so he was put in charge of making a big enough handle and turning it fast enough to supply a town. Apparently, this had not proven to be easy until the relative had spotted a boat moored nearby. He talked the firm into buying it and they pulled it backwards up a slipway until the propeller was clear of the water. Then, when he attached the handle to the propeller, they had all the power they needed, all they had to do was couple the cables together to connect the town.

No-one ever admitted to it, but someone asked "So at last one of your lot got the credit then?"

Percy slumped "No, we were never wealthy and he was electrocuted trying to make ends meet."

When someone knocked on Cuthbert's door, it always caused an invisible panic inside Cuthbert's head, because good news never came that way, but this knocking was in stereo, it was coming from the walls as well and if the panic could have moved faster, it would have reached his limbs and perhaps activated a reaction. All this was avoided by some of the women entering through the front door and Margery coming through a door in the wall.

Seeing Cuthbert's lack of expression, Margery sighed, "You moan if I don't knock Cuthbert what do you want me to do now, whistle?"

"Yes?" asked a hooded figure in the corner sitting by the pot plant.

The room was filling up rapidly and Arkle had dragged a hay bale into the room because Cuthbert's chairs weren't quite saddle-shaped enough for her.

"Oh dear, you've turned Cuthbert's kitchen into a stable," giggled Elspeth.

Arkle snorted, further reinforcing the impression of being in a stable, "I wouldn't put any of my horses in this dump, they are used to the basics at least," she said.

Percy just had to give in to his inner self-destructiveness and he smirked as he commented, "Perhaps stables wouldn't be so scruffy if the horses took their shoes off Ar..."

Perhaps the smirk had caused the lack of concentration and he froze as Arkle growled "Arr?"

Percy looked around desperately, but the room was full of people and the exits were blocked. His life began to flash before him so he had a few hours left on that basis alone.

Margery came to the rescue yet again with "*Are* you sitting comfortably dear? We worry about you with mites and ticks from the hay."

Arkle slowly panned her gaze from Percy to Cuthbert and back again before hissing, "Oh I'm immune to mites and ticks Margery, right up to the point where I crush them."

Her audience gulped.

The men had thought that the purpose of this meeting at Cuthbert's had been to drink dreadful coffee and escape from the women, but the women were now explaining that it was actually to discuss whether the new police station should be a concern and would it cause problems for anyone with a past. A silence settled as each of them analysed a life misspent.

Percy was pretty much an accidental tourist when it came to crime, things just seemed to happen around him and they could hardly jail him for all the adventures of his ancestors unless the ancestors of the policemen were still alive now could they?

Cuthbert didn't have much of a conscience either, because he didn't really notice when things went wrong, and anyway he usually buried his mistakes.

Ronald of course was a different matter to everyone else. He had been involved in every murky plot and insurrection around the world during the last twenty years, but everyone who could cause him problems was either deceased, fled, paid off or elected to high government office and they didn't want to lose their perks.

Henry of course had been a famous news reporter who had fed off his brother, Ronald's tip-offs whilst staying in the best hotels enjoying the view from the roof, while he sat in ejector seats salvaged from crashed aircraft sipping whatever available mixture passed for a cocktail. The only real dangers were the ingredients of the cocktails and accidentally pressing the wrong button on the seat and ending up several countries away.

The Captain had experienced a long and fruitful military career, or it might have been, if he could remember much of it. Somehow, he had the Khyber Pass mixed up with the Boer War and The Indian Mutiny, if anyone ever worked out the timeline he may be in line for an extra pension.

Even Whistle had a guilty secret, he had agreed to sell all the fish he caught from the reservoir with no water to the fishmonger in the next Valley, but at the moment he was distracted, wondering how the pot plant beside him was managing to steal his crisps.

The women were equally engrossed in preparations for damage limitation should this Chief Inspector prove to be over-zealous.

Margery of course had run the Valley mafia whilst posing as the put upon mother of the twins, but she had covered her tracks very well and was now the legitimate co-owner of the Mandrake Arms with her husband Henry.

Of course the fact that Jasper had found a way to open the 'Tamper-proof' beer barrels and sometimes they became accidentally diluted, may cause concern and the regular ambushes of the crisp truck before it reached the other valleys may have to be scaled back.

Margery sighed; she had been putting off checking the provenance of the meat pies and pasties for as long as she could but now...

Arkle was feeling slightly uncomfortable but the hay bale wasn't causing it; she only had to wriggle once and her shape stayed there forever like a fossil.

The source of her discomfort was her highly successful record as a racehorse owner in the past. Liberal use of spray paint and different shaped templates had allowed her to enter previously unregistered horses with only an outside chance with the bookies. It had been quite lucrative and at least she had never drugged her animals, she didn't need to, they were terrified of her.

Elspeth had seen the world by accompanying her husband, the Captain and she would often think back to her adventures. She had a wonderful collection of jewels in a safety deposit box, but highway robbery didn't count as a crime here if it took place on a dirt track abroad did it?

As an archaeologist, Geraldine was used to digging through dirt to find one small useful piece to further her career and pass her exams. She smiled to herself as she remembered the reaction to her paper on the Roman occupation of Britain. She had salted the ground with so many artefacts borrowed from museums that colleagues actually believed that the Romans had been here.

Avril, the local reporter for the Triple Echo was sure that she had a clear conscience; just look at her, stuck writing for a local rag where nothing happened and if it did, she wasn't allowed to print it due to local pressure, surely that was proof that she was an incorruptible servant of the media? Then it struck her, it meant the very opposite, she had compromised her journalistic integrity and suppressed the news, she was no better than any of these other reprobates she thought as Cuthbert and Percy swam into her teary vision.

The pot plant in the corner trembled as Jasper ate the last of Whistle's crisps and he smiled to himself. All these adults worried to death about their tiny misdemeanours and he was untouchable, he was too young to prosecute. Hang on, he thought, how old am I?

The road gang were also having a brief moment of introspection as the concrete foundation was being poured.

The Valley mafia had kindly donated the deflated and rolled up bouncy castle to plug the hole and stop the concrete from escaping into the tunnels.

Marvin and his team regarded this as a noble act whilst completely missing the point that it would allow the mafia access into the new police station basement when it was removed. Marvin had accompanied his road works team because the cost of replacing lost equipment was crippling his department and there were rumours of stalls on car boot sales making a tidy profit.

Marvin watched as the truck poured the grey sludge from its rotating drum like a giant snail, he saw the sludge self-level and the occasional air bubble 'pop' on its surface. Perhaps, this was how life

34

began he thought, a primordial soup from which creatures emerged. Glancing sideways, he saw the road gang and giggled involuntarily before returning to his thoughts.

The road gang glanced at Marvin suspiciously before they also returned to their own thoughts. If they had compared notes, it would have been obvious that the same thought was running through everyone's head today, 'What does this new police station mean to me and should I be worried?'

Marvin chewed his bottom lip; it was never easy to reach the dizzy heights of the Local Authority and corners had to be cut and intelligence gathered along the way.

He had never knowingly done anything illegal, but surely it had been his duty to report the Mayor for having different tyre pressures on his car even if it had been Marvin who had 'adjusted' them?

Of course, he was in no doubt that his actions had been correct when the mayoral chain went missing and Marvin reported seeing it in a pawn shop window.

They never did find the man of Marvin's height and build, but with a moustache and beard who had pawned it; but the Mayor was obviously not suited to the job and everybody moved one more rung up the ladder.

The drains inspector really resented Marvin being here to supervise them, especially as he stayed upwind of his team.

Any other time, the Valley mafia would have been all over their equipment like locusts, but today all they cared about was stopping the concrete from being wasted.

Strange little chaps, he thought, before wracking his brains for misdemeanours which may be lurking in his past.

Drains inspectors aren't made of course, they are forged in the white-hot furnace of experience, they do not come ready programmed with the knowledge of stop valves, one way valves and non-return valves, it was a life-long learning process and some were lost along the way.

Of course, that may actually be his downfall, the manner in which they had been lost along the way. His first superior had been lost in a whirlpool, after a person or persons unknown opened a sluice valve; the second one had been sucked into a rubber hose which bulged like a python trying to swallow a cow before being ejected at high speed into the next county; the third in line as his superior, had quit on the basis of things that had happened to the other two and so a new, accident free drains inspector was born.

Now, 'swivelling Simon' couldn't actually remember what had happened to his eye and there was no family alive to tell him, but whereas many may claim it to be a liability, Simon had found several advantages to it. For instance, if he wanted to appear solid and reliable, he kept both eyes staring resolutely ahead, but if he wanted to distract or disconcert someone, he would roll the real eye and stumble to give the impression that the zombie apocalypse had begun. The only blot on his record was when he was accused of shoplifting. He had been reprieved when he pointed out that when he bought a pair of socks, he could only see one of them and he often left the other one behind, so he wasn't actually stealing, he was in fact leaving.

The management accepted this with their apologies, but the security guard and Simon both swore to keep an eye on each other from then on.

'One lung Louie' was similar to the Captain; he had given so many explanations for his condition that he could no longer remember which one was the truth. They varied from 'Being gassed in The Great War' to 'Second hand smoke' when he was a chimney sweep and even 'Damaged, diving too deep whilst trying to raise the Titanic.' His timelines were no better than the Captain's, either.

Now Buster was a simple soul, a "gentle giant," they said, "Wouldn't harm a fly," they said, but according to the FBI (Flies Bureau of Investigation,) he was a rampant serial killer and their SWAT team had him in their sights.

The sudden silence shook everyone from their reveries as the truck finished pouring and the new foundation lay before them, was it a new beginning or the beginning of something new? This was the Valley after all.

Jasper called the meeting to order, he was pleased that his ruse had worked and after pulling the bouncy castle chrysalis out of the hole, they now had a secret access to the police station's basement or cells, or whatever it turned out to be. They were several steps ahead of the adults as usual, and that's just where the mafia liked to be.

Chapter Twelve

The population of Cuthbert's kitchen had decided to congregate again at the Mandrake Arms and they all meandered past the site of the new police station where Constable Beeching stood apparently on guard with his thumbs tucked into his uniform jacket front.

"Watcha copper" said Percy brightly.

The officer glared at Percy, "Don't try it on with me feller me lad, I'm on duty." And his stare returned to the middle distance.

"So, watcha doin'?" continued Percy deliberately goading him.

The constable took a deep breath and replied "I am standing guard over the police station to make sure that those nincompoops living in the Valley don't do anything to compromise its integrity before it is even integrated." His expression betrayed the fact that passing on that little speech had made his head hurt.

Percy gasped, "But you're too late mate, it's gone."

The dedicated guardian fought to keep his eyes forward and resist the urge to check on Percy's obviously ridiculous statement, "No it hasn't," he squawked.

The crowd building up behind Percy all nodded like a pantomime audience as they chanted "Oh yes it has."

Beads of sweat appeared on Constable Beeching's forehead as he tried to assess the quality of this information, he didn't trust most of the Valley, but that nice Margery was there and the newspaper reporter as well. He turned quickly and tried to quell the panic, they were right, it had gone!

Margery could stand it no longer, she tapped Beeching's sleeve and said, "They haven't built it yet, Constable, it's *the site* they sent you to guard."

Constable Beeching glared and tried to find a retort as the crowd dispersed giggling. It wasn't his fault that he followed orders, he didn't expect to actually check them as well. At last, he remembered something that would teach them to taunt an officer of the law, "You lot won't be so smug when the speed cameras are erected." He smirked as everyone drifted back; he had their attention now all right.

"What speed cameras?" Henry asked.

The constable couldn't hide his delight, "The one's we're putting in next week, then you'll see who is in charge."

Henry exchanged glances with several of the people nearest to him before he said, "But this is the Valley, *you're the only one with a car.*"

"Oh," said the constable.

* * *

The Chief Constable tapped a pencil on his desk, he had been up all night going through Beeching's crime reports for the umpteenth time and whilst he had used them to present his case and panic the commissioners into authorising the new police station, he had a feeling that some of the pitched battles the constable had allegedly fought, didn't actually match the physique of the man.

One man vehicle checkpoint, yes, he could block a road without putting barriers up, but chasing his own car to wrench it back from the thieves?

The pencil tapped faster and faster, no-one would take his first command away from him, he would need a specialist team for this outpost of the law. He would only be satisfied when the Valley became 'no-man's land,' because when there were no men in it, peace would reign.

Then he remembered Arkle and gave a shudder. Pressing a button on his intercom, he snapped, "Get me personnel immediately." The interviews need to be scheduled and supervised as soon as possible.

* * *

The atmosphere in the Mandrake Arms was an odd one. Whilst the occupants dreaded change, they also relished adventure and things could become boring to the point where they finished each other's sentences and that could be really disconcerting sat around Cuthbert's table when voices were heard, but the wrong lips were moving. It was like a ventriloquist's convention at times.

* * *

38

Cuthbert hadn't gone with the others; he was still desperately trying to find an unknown play, so that he controlled the performance, instead of some upstart, who actually knew what he was talking about.

He had left the door open on the cooking range and any scraps of paper or cobweb cities were simply thrown into the flames.

The last parchment had looked promising, but as usual, the writing looked like a spider had crawled into an inkwell and staggered off across the paper to die.

Cuthbert peered at it closely and sighed; he could make out the word 'Bacon' right at the bottom above a wax seal. 'Just another shopping list,' he thought and pushed it into the hungry flames where it writhed and crackled in an attempt to make some fool recognise a masterpiece when they saw it, then it gave up and crumpled, ashes to ashes eh?

As a last resort, the wax seal detached itself and slipped onto the floor before it could melt.

Cuthbert rummaged away behind another set of panelling oblivious to it all.

Chapter Thirteen

The first recruit the Chief Inspector needed, was a first-rate desk sergeant; one who could assess the public the moment they walked in and reassure them that even though there were no results, everything possible was being done. He also had to be au fait with police procedural systems, so that even when everyone was asleep, he would at least know where they were. He had scribbled down a series of interview questions, psychologically calculated to select only the best, but after testing them on anyone passing his office, he only got as far as, "Could you imagine yourself working in a Valley environment?" and the pretend candidate fled.

* * *

Margery had resigned herself to changing the light bulb in the back room, because even though there was a bar full of men, the fluidity of job titles in the Valley could be quite baffling; husbands became customers and were therefore exempt from any manual labour until their glasses were empty and at a shout of "my round chaps," they promptly exempted themselves even further.

Just at that moment, Percy appeared and sauntered over to Margery with his screwdrivers tucked into his turned down wellies, he was obviously in handy-man mode, so Margery poured him a pint in anticipation of assistance and he downed it gratefully.

"What's that?" asked Percy surveying Margery's preparations for the job in hand.

"It's my stepladder" said Margery proudly.

Percy looked stricken and his shoulders slumped.

"Whatever's wrong Percy?" asked Margery really quite worried about this sudden change.

Percy sniffed, "I had a stepladder once, I never knew my real ladder" and he slowly left the room with his shoulders slumped.

Margery stared after him in amazement and seeing the empty glass, she looked around wildly to see if anyone, anyone at all could explain to her what had just happened.

* * *

The Chief Inspector was baffled. He had authorised internal memos advertising the available posts at the new police station and distributed leaflets to put on notice boards for miles around. The problem seemed to be a subliminal one; the more he tried to hide the location of the new post, the more it crept into the script. For instance, the one for his Personal Assistant read 'Very Able Liaison Lady Enthusiastic and Young required.' But all anyone could see was 'Valley,' they must be psychic he thought.

The one for quick response team drivers had similar problems with 'Vehicle Arrests Limiting Larcenous Enterprises and Yobs, rare opportunity for drivers.'

There must be a better way to recruit staff, he thought. Perhaps, he should try a ceramics factory, seeing as he needed a load of mugs.

The Police Commissioner swept down the corridors of his training establishment, glancing into any reflective surface as he went. He was proud of his post and his uniform, with all its silver attachments. He had even bought a miniature vacuum cleaner to keep the braid in pristine condition in case someone influential was arrested and he had to be involved in a scuffle before the cameras.

Turning the last corner before his office, he stopped, he gasped and his heart invented a whole new rhythm.

There, sitting in the corridor were three young constables, all straight backed and holding their truncheons at the regulation position vertically before them.

Glancing around for an escape route, the Commissioner saw the notice board and spotted a new job opportunity pinned to it. Snatching the sheet of paper, he focused upon the future and headed towards the most challenging recruits he had ever met.

Sitting at his desk, The Commissioner removed his hat and laid it pointing towards the door as if the braid would ward off evil spirits.

The three constables stood before him were rigidly at attention and still held their truncheons vertically in front of them. Even though everyone one else had been trained in telescopic batons, pepper sprays and even firearms, these three had shown that the traditional blunt instrument was much safer, especially for those around them.

The instructor who had tried every tactic he knew for self-defence with a truncheon, resigned in tears, claiming that they were Morris Dancers trying to infiltrate the force. He had almost been sacked himself after setting the dogs on them, but they simply threw their truncheons and the dogs retrieved them.

The Commissioner took a deep breath and pushed the piece of paper closer to the three new recruits in front of him. "There is a rare opportunity to be in on the ground floor of a new police building in a criminal hot-spot. It has been specially designed for withstanding a siege and allowing the use of snatch squads to isolate the troublemakers. If you are interested, then your future is assured, if you are not interested then you will be transferred to Antarctica directing penguin traffic jams."

The three heads opposite the head's, nodded slowly in unison and the Commissioner relaxed. He was about to dismiss them when a thought occurred to him, "Why were you sent to see me anyway?" he asked.

The middle constable of the trio hesitated before replying, "We were caught playing cards sir."

The Commissioner's mood was lifting by the second as he realised that these three would soon be off his hands, so he sportingly asked, "Who was winning?"

The right-hand constable said brightly, "Oh I was sir; I had just swapped The Artful Dodger for Nick Leeson."

Their superior was puzzled, "I don't know that game; what is it called?"

The left-hand constable supplied, "Rogue Traders, sir."

The celebrations at the training establishment were usually quite a muted and professional affair, but at this news, the whole place erupted and a gala atmosphere ensued, the odd thing was that the three constables were not invited.

Chapter Fourteen

Members of the Valley theatre group had been invited over to Cuthbert's kitchen to discuss his findings, which mostly consisted of scraps of parchment heaped up on the kitchen table.

Geraldine seemed to be the only one able to translate the handwriting, but of course as the museum's curator she had the experience, especially after trying to decipher her predecessor's records. She sighed and skimmed another yellowed sheet across the table where it took flight and landed near to the cooking range. Bending to retrieve it, Geraldine scooped up a wax disc from nearby and gasped. "Where did this come from Cuthbert?" she asked breathlessly.

Cuthbert shrugged and explained about the several inches thick pile of shopping lists he had burned. He was particularly proud of his skill in reading the word bacon and was sure that his skills would equal Geraldine's.

"You idiot!" shrieked Geraldine, "Do you know what you've done?"

Now, Cuthbert *never* knew what he'd done, all he knew was that every time something happened, he was never very far away and someone was looking at him the way Geraldine was right now.

Geraldine held the wax disc in one hand and stroked it reverentially with the other, "This," she breathed, "is the wax seal showing the coat of arms of Sir Francis Bacon, a sixteenth century Gentleman playwright who may have even written the plays we attribute to Shakespeare."

"Phew," said Percy, "That was close, at least it wasn't the real thing; this must be one of the rasher things Cuthbert's done yet."

He looked around waiting for a reaction, but he was met by looks of hostility, until Ronald accidentally distracted everyone with, "Was he the one who stole Christopher Columbus's furniture?"

"No," snapped Geraldine, "That was Sir Francis Drake," clenching her fists under the table.

Henry shrugged "I thought he looked after all the animals."

43

"That was Saint Francis of Assisi," screamed Geraldine before adding, "Philistines, I'm surrounded by Philistines."

"Are they the ones who…" began Percy, but Geraldine swept the pile of parchments across the room and stormed out.

Henry broke the silence with, "Well, Cuthbert whatever play you decide on, Geraldine would be perfect for one of the Furies."

* * *

Chief Inspector Peebles sat behind his desk and stared at his new team, he knew his colleagues at the training establishment quite well and he pretty well knew why he had inherited this trio. The three constables stood to attention and held old-fashioned wooden truncheons firmly in front of them, no-one moved. Checking the paperwork before him, the superior officer asked, "So, you all have the same surname and live within a few miles of each other, but you are not related?"

Three heads nodded slowly in recognition of this.

"Did one of your fathers have a bike?" he tried in an attempt at levity, but he was met by blank stares.

"Well," he continued, "Constables Pickles, we may have trouble telling you apart, but you are certainly welcome on the team, in fact you *are* the team."

The constables straightened their backs and gripped and then gripped the truncheons a little tighter. This was it, they were on front-line duty.

* * *

Percy usually dawdled at the back when the others wandered into town but this time he was sitting on the horse trough waiting for the others to catch up when the police car pulled up.

The Chief Inspector got out from the driving seat and three identical constables unfolded themselves from the back seat before standing rigidly to attention, holding their truncheons before them.

Percy gaped and looked around to see who had set this up for him, the opportunities were endless. His brain began to spin and he almost fell into the trough.

44

The Chief Inspector was pacing up and down and addressing the three rigid upholders of the law, "Take in your surroundings gentlemen, the tranquillity is deceptive, this Valley is a hotbed of crime and criminal enterprise. I have to interview the landlady at the local Inn, use your time wisely," and with that he walked away.

Percy wandered casually over and inspected 'his' troops, noticing that one of the officers glanced at him and whispered, "Bye-law infringement four-six-two," causing another one to also glance and mutter "With sub-section twelve, of course." The third one nodded in agreement.

Percy was adept at ignoring most things especially when he didn't know what they meant. One thing he did understand was the 'cut-throat' gesture and thumbs-up given to him by Jasper, as the Valley mafia closed in on the police car behind the uniformed version of The Terracotta Warriors.

"One of my ancestors was in law enforcement, you know," Percy began, giving a cough to mask a hub-cap clanking carelessly to the ground.

The faces of the constables remained rigid and Percy sensed a challenge. "Of course, it wasn't here; my ancestor emigrated to America at the time of the Wild West and knew all the gunslingers. Have you heard of Billy the Kid?"

The constable in the centre, nodded in spite of himself, so Percy continued.

"Heard of Wild Bill Hickock then?"

He was rewarded by two reluctant nods so he tried, "Marshall Penelope Plumm?" but it brought no reaction at all, "Not surprised, really," said Percy "Women weren't taken very seriously back then, but it worked in her favour because even though no-one would sell her a gun, she could always buy some rope and say it was a washing line.

Very often, the crooks woke up in the cells trussed up like turkeys with the local lawman taking all the credit, because these tough outlaws wouldn't admit to being caught by a woman with a rope and a slip-knot, even though they knew she was the lass-oo caught them."

The constables were looking straight at him now and the truncheons were drooping slightly, so he added, "Even Ben Franklin owed his discovery of electricity to her, because he borrowed her rope for his kite."

One of the constables was so impressed that he turned to the car where he'd left his notebook, but as he dropped his truncheon in shock, he realised that the book was the least of his worries. The car was just a shell standing on blocks.

He turned back to Percy who shrugged and said "You can always buy the bits back, but they'll charge you for the blocks as well."

Just then, Henry walked by and seeing the looks on the faces of the three officers he asked, "You've met Percy then?"

Beside him, Margery squeezed his arm and said "Aaah bless, they're brand new, have they opened a new box?"

Another sound caused the policemen to turn in the opposite direction as the road gang lined up behind them and One-lung Louie emitted his trademark "Hurr-hurr-hurr," whilst pointing at the remains of the police car. "Did nobody warn you about this place?" he asked smirking, until Buster queried, "Where's our van?"

* * *

The Chief Inspector had waited patiently for Margery and Henry to return.

Patiently, in his case meant checking the cupboards, the till receipts and the seals on the barrels. He knew a crooked establishment when he saw it and the only explanation for the roles these local characters played was the acting skills they had picked up over the years, it never occurred to him that he had not seen one of their plays yet.

Henry entered and greeted him warmly enough before he went behind the bar to offer him a drink, but Margery's eyes darted around the place as if she had thermal recognition and she could see the fading heat from his fingerprints everywhere.

The inspector narrowed his eyes; he would have to watch this one.

After the usual questions involving how long Margery and Henry had lived there and whether business was good, the Chief Inspector paused before asking some leading questions about the locals.

He frowned at the sound of three pairs of boots crashing into the bar and he turned to see his three constables stood in a row with

46

truncheons held before them, "What is it?" he snapped, irritated at the interruption.

The left-hand constable spluttered "The car sir, it's gone."

The middle constable added, "Well, not all of it sir."

The right-hand constable concluded, "But most of it has sir."

The senior officer leapt to his feet and dashed outside where he joined the road gang and they all seemed to compete in a 'who looks the most puzzled' contest.

"Did you see what happened?" the officer demanded.

"Er no," replied the drains inspector guardedly, "but I'd like to report a stolen van while you're here."

Margery bit her lip as she watched from the window, "I'm not sure about him at all," she muttered. "Coming to a backwater like this, he wants to make a name for himself, it could be dangerous."

Henry made light of it, "Oh come on dear, he's just a typical policeman, unless it happens under his nose, it doesn't register."

Margery sighed, "Darling husband, the mafia have just dismantled his police car and left it on blocks forcing him to walk home, if that isn't under his nose, I don't know what is."

Henry shrugged, "At least he wasn't interested in us, dear."

Margery sighed again and went around all the cupboards and drawers, showing Henry the snapped hairs she had glued across them before going out.

"Oh," said Henry.

Margery then smiled her delicate, but deadly smile as she added, "And there's also one on the bottle-top of the whiskey bottle under the bar dear."

"Oh," said Henry again.

Chapter Fifteen

The Chief Inspector and his three trusty constables began the long walk home, pretending that it was a routine exercise, by inspecting doors and windows along the way. The Chief Inspector's blushes had been partly hidden now after surprising Mrs Biggle as she left a friend's house and she covered him in 'midnight blush' from her powder compact, thinking he was an intruder and trying to phone the very police who stood before her.

The road gang had assembled outside Marvin's office and they were addressing the partly open window because they were still not allowed inside due to the nature of their occasional forays into the drainage and sewage systems and the drifting aroma it left trailing behind them.

The drains inspector had pleaded the case for another van on the basis of "Even the police couldn't defend their own vehicle and they were armed."

Marvin was appalled, "Good Lord," he spluttered, "Do you want to be issued with guns now?"

He was even more appalled at the following silence whilst the team considered his offer.

Jasper had not been able to hide behind the pot plant and listen in when the Chief Inspector had visited, because some of the younger members were still being trained in the art of high speed dismantling of wheeled vehicles, but he had high hopes for them. He sipped his orange juice in the bar as Margery shared her reservations about having the police in the Valley.

Jasper asked, "Where did he get the three stooges from and why do they carry rolling pins around with them?"

Margery shrugged, it must have been difficult to recruit staff for the Valley so they were probably *special* constables. They both giggled at this.

* * *

48

Geraldine was checking the ancient weapons in the museum storage rooms, there had to be a way to get rid of Cuthbert and gain access to his farm, then she could tear it apart and find any other unknown manuscripts, before the dolt made papier-mâché' landscapes out of them, or Percy used them for insoles in his wellies.

Moving the wooden handled spears apart, her fingers caressed the Amazonian blow-pipe someone had donated years ago. Easily concealed, silent and deadly, and she even had some darts.

In another section of the museum, there were old books detailing poisons, so the means and methods were all here and they could not be traced back to her. She sniggered, life was so rewarding when it had a purpose.

Chapter Sixteen

The Bricklayers had never been in the Valley before, but the wages were so tempting they hadn't thought to ask questions. Anyway, because it was a police station there was a uniformed presence at all times and even a drainage team in attendance, although they didn't seem to move far from their own van.

There was a slight anomaly there which should have caused concern because the council road works van actually looked like an old ice-cream van; it even had an illuminated cornet on top with a chocolate flake in it. However, the drains inspector seemed fond enough of it, because he never left its side, mostly because he knew that Marvin was running out of suppliers.

The bricklayers erected a little tent and started the day with a cup of tea which almost caused a rebellion amongst the road gang because there was room to carry their digging equipment but no room for a stove and kettle. Plus, with them all in the back, every time Buster flexed his muscles, it set the chimes off.

The brickies eventually started work and were handing stacks of bricks down into the hole for the foundations. As professionals, they automatically counted each brick and then each pile as it was passed and stacked, but suddenly the stacks in the hole didn't seem to be increasing at the rate they were leaving the flat-backed truck.

The foreman called a halt and announced his professional appraisal, "There's something funny going on here," he said looking suspiciously at the road gang who had formed a cordon around their ice-cream van and were very alert indeed.

One of the brickies pointed at one of the side walls of the hole and asked, "Did that wall just move?"

Jasper practiced an adult curse and shook his head, they had been slow in letting the rubber wall made from the bouncy castle fall back into place and even though it was perfectly camouflaged, the workman had seen the movement.

Most of the stolen bricks had been whisked away down the tunnels, but they still needed more to build the Mayor's double garage in the next valley, "Quick, cause a distraction," he hissed and one of his 'men' left by a back exit.

The brickies were closing in on the suspect piece of earth and were poking and tapping their way towards it from both sides when a voice called "Help, Help!" It sounded desperate, so the workmen climbed out of the foundations to join the three constables by their builders' truck.

"What is it lad?" asked the foreman when he saw a boy writhing on the ground half under his truck.

"You ran over me," accused the boy.

The foreman looked at the truck, then at the boy and helped him up giving him a good natured clip around the ear in fun. "Get away with you," he grinned.

The lad promptly collapsed and began writhing on the ground again shouting, but this time, "Help, Police, he hit me and opened up all the wounds he caused by running over me."

The foreman gaped as the three constables surrounded him and the left-hand constable said, "You are under arrest."

The middle-constable added, "Anything you say will be taken down."

The right hand constable finished with, "And be used in evidence against you."

All the sudden fuss was like a magnet and a crowd had formed now with Margery shouting, "Shame on you, look how young he is."

Elspeth shouted, "Throw the book at him officers."

One of the workmen shouted, "Where did the rest of the bricks go?"

The drains inspector shouted, "Where's our van?"

Mrs Biggle simply covered everyone in 'powdered bliss' while she called for reinforcements.

Jasper was impressed, that was some distraction; he'd have to keep an eye on that one.

Marvin had quite a crowd outside his window now, and between all the shouting between the road gang and the bricklayers, all he could assume was that he would need another van.

* * *

51

The three constables stood before the Chief Inspector, rigidly at attention and with truncheons ready.

He looked at each one of them in turn, "Did any of you strike the foreman bricklayer?" he asked quietly whilst pointedly eyeing the truncheons, "because he had three bumps on his head when you brought him in."

"Certainly not sir," said the left-hand constable.

"Definitely not sir," added the middle constable.

"No need to sir," said the right-hand constable finally.

Their superior raised an eyebrow, "No need?" he asked curiously.

"I've started Karate lessons sir," said the left-hand constable.

"I've started Taekwondo lessons sir," said the middle constable.

"I've started Judo lessons sir," added the right-hand constable.

The Chief Inspector sighed, "So now you are all partial arts experts are you?"

The constables nodded slowly to their superior as they would have to the Sensei in their local dojo.

"Give the foreman a lift home and don't let him see those antique clubs or his memory may start coming back" and with a wave of his hand he dismissed them.

Chapter Seventeen

The site of the new police station resembled Rorke's Drift the next day with all lorries and vans drawn up into a laager formation for mutual protection and extra guards facing outwards.

The constables were patrolling and trying to avoid the foreman who was rubbing the bumps on his head and looking puzzled.

As the first bricks were laid, everyone seemed to relax and assume that the job would proceed peacefully now and only the kerchunk of the cement mixer and the scrape of trowels could be heard.

One of the constables scowled as he spotted a cloud of black smoke coming from the direction of Cuthbert's farm and he pointed it out to the others.

After a quick consultation, the constables agreed that it was getting closer and they carried out a risk assessment of the site.

All guards were instructed to hide behind the lorries, whilst the brickies carried on working because they were down in the hole and the bricks were above head-height now, so they were behind a barrier.

The smoke was getting closer and they could even feel the ground beginning to shake. After a last look around, one of the constables recognised the harmless old sheepdog which never seemed to move, so he tried to entice him away from the road, but the dog didn't seem to notice him. The only option left was to push the animal clear from behind and that's when blind Pugh became a whirling dervish.

The constable screamed and ran into the road straight into the path of Percy's tractor. Percy pulled a lever and locked one of the tracks, causing the machine to slew across the road, only to demolish the rented council van and leap the gap before coming to rest on a pile of bricks which had previously been a brand new wall.

Percy pushed his goggles up onto his head and looked around at the chaos, "Ooops!" he said.

* * *

The Chief Inspector now had his Personal Assistant and she was stood right in front of him looking like a recruiting poster for Women police officers everywhere. Everything was perfect and she had already researched him and sent flowers for his wife's birthday. She had that natural presence needed to control unruly journalists at a sensitive press conference where she would distract the men very nicely and that would only leave the women who might actually be listening.

He signed the papers laid before him and thanked her for his coffee. Before she left the office, he thought, WPC Hannah Cuffs would complete his team and he would introduce her to the Valley today.

* * *

Percy had rescued his tractor and wrecked all the other brickwork in the attempt, so he headed for The Mandrake Arms where the bar was full but silent.

The Chief Inspector seemed to have that effect upon the socialising public and his new companion didn't help.

Margery watched as Percy came in and flattened his hair with the damp cloth she had just wiped the soggy bar with and she sighed, Percy was smitten again.

The WPC was beside her boss ready to take notes and carefully scanning the bar for known, unknown or future suspects when she sensed a presence beside her and mentally shut down before her analytical mind could suffer from eye contact.

"Can I buy you a drink?" Percy simpered.

This claimed the attention of the whole bar because Percy had never paid for anything and they could only dread to think where he kept his money.

The woman officer smiled and replied, "Only if you offer me something you can't pronounce."

Percy hesitated, then paused and then hesitated again, oh, this one was smart he thought, time for some sophistication.

"We could use that secluded booth in the corner and get to know each other better," he tried. To his amazement, the officer nodded and took a seat at the corner table and Percy joined her, without mentioning a drink of course.

Percy began his campaign with, "Has anyone told you that I'm the man to go to in the Valley? Nothing gets past me because my ancestors were warriors and we Plumm's are constantly alert."

The WPC heard a snigger and made a mental note to check out the pot plant behind her. "So you have an impressive family tree then Percy?"

Percy puffed out his chest, she already knew his first name; this was going to be easy

"Oh yes," he began, "We were with Drake at the Armada, Nelson at Trafalgar and Wellington at Waterloo."

Giving a disdainful sniff, Hannah glanced down at Percy's footwear, "Did you inherit them then?"

"Inherit what?" asked Percy.

"The Wellingtons, they certainly smell like heirlooms."

Percy had a vague sense that he wasn't in control here, especially when his companion announced.

"My lineage isn't so much a family tree, more of a family vine, our vineyard produced some of the finest grapes in the region, but we were especially renowned for our Plumm Brandy."

Percy frowned, he could have sworn that she had pronounced it with two m's on the end. "Plum brandy?" he asked.

"Oh no," said Hannah with a reptilian smile. "Plumm Brandy, my mother used to round up all the children named Plumm and put them through the grape press. Do you have children Percy?"

Percy gulped.

Leaving Percy with a shaking and silently hysterical pot plant, the WPC went back to stand beside her boss at the bar where Margery asked mischievously "Are you and Percy engaged yet?"

Hannah smirked, "No but we have an arrangement."

* * *

The bricklayers had begun to suspect that there was something odd about this Valley and they were working faster than ever. There was nothing like moving bushes, disappearing bricks and a bus hurtling past covered in sheepskin rugs to focus the mind. The brickwork was coming along a treat, but there was a long way to go yet before this state of the art oasis of legislation would be in action against the dark and unseen forces of the Valley.

Police Constable Beeching sat in his patrol car hidden behind a large bush and contemplated the changes being made around him. As he munched on his pizza and remembered the reports he had sent in to headquarters, he smiled to himself. All these reinforcements would come in handy and he would make sure that everyone got to the scene of the crime before him.

The mafia would regret the way they had treated him over the years and that Percy could look out too. He tore off another portion and chewed contentedly.

Jasper watched as Constable Colossus sat and ate his supper. Surely the clot realised that he would have to move into the new police station and justify his existence? Sighing at the predictable short-sightedness of adults, he waved his men forward.

Chapter Eighteen

Cuthbert had been subjected to a tirade from Percy after he had returned home and slammed the door twice for emphasis. It was something about handcuffs and plum brandy. Perhaps his friend had gone to a blind tasting and they'd handcuffed him to stop him from pouring samples into his wellies again.

The two friends knew each other so well that the words just hummed around Cuthbert as he went to close the door, which had bounced open in objection to its mistreatment.

As he closed it, something else hummed through the gap and Percy suddenly went quiet behind him.

Cuthbert turned and there was his friend, fast asleep across the table.

Outside, Geraldine cursed and pushed another dart into the blowpipe. Should she wait behind the wall or use the tunnels to enter secretly, because there was neither rhyme nor reason to Cuthbert's movements and she could be here all night.

She headed uphill towards the reservoir, where she could enter the tunnels only to find her way blocked by Ronald and Whistle.

Ronald had been lying low since the police began appearing in the Valley. As an ex-mercenary, he was prepared to face the charges of inciting distant battles and misappropriation of Government ammunition, but he wasn't prepared to go to prison for an old parking ticket he had forgotten about, so he had taken to the great outdoors and was spending time with Whistle arguing about battles with unruly tribesmen compared to battles with non-existent fish.

Geraldine had never been the most patient of people and these two were getting on her nerves. Even her four year qualifying exams only took two thanks to industrial scale cheating. She readied the blow-gun and took aim.

Ronald's tactical senses were tingling, the slight rustle in the undergrowth, the sigh of the wind stopping as someone blocked its passage, but it was the thud at the back of his neck which convinced him that he had been right as he fell flat on his face.

Whistle didn't even notice, because the dart simply lodged in his hood and he had nodded off anyway.

Geraldine moved slowly forward and checked Ronald's pockets where she acquired a knife, a knuckle-duster and some glow sticks. Feeling like a ninja, she dropped into the hole and headed downhill for Cuthbert's farm.

* * *

The Chief Inspector was savouring his coffee and discussing the day with WPC Hannah Cuffs. "You seemed to handle that Percy chap well enough," he said admiringly. "What did you make of the others?"

The officer considered this before replying, "The Percy's of this world are no problem; you just have to show them that you are more insane than they are.

Henry seems innocent enough, he's simply settled down for an easy life in the worst possible place he could have chosen."

She paused before adding, "Now Margery gives off some mixed signals, there's a secret there somewhere and she cultivates some very strange house plants, but it's the ex-mercenary Ronald and this Cuthbert chap I would really like to meet."

Her boss nodded, she had hit the nail on the head. "Well, that's tomorrows visit arranged then."

* * *

Cuthbert was in a quandary. He normally didn't notice, but this time everyone kept saying, "You're in a quandary Cuthbert" and he had begun to believe it.

Early this morning, the mafia had turned up at his door with Ronald in a wheelbarrow and tipped him onto the kitchen floor.

Jasper was really concerned, because someone had rifled the pockets before they had got there. "You'd better put him with the other stiffs Cuthbert," he said as he left.

"What other stiffs?" asked Cuthbert as business was slow lately.

Just then, Percy slid down off the table and onto the floor with a thud.

By the time the Captain and Henry had arrived, the two bodies were laid out in Cuthbert's outbuilding and he was reading the embalming manual whilst he had a cup of tea.

"Are you sure they're dead Cuthbert?" asked Henry suspiciously.

Cuthbert paused with the cup half-way to his lips, "Does it say 'Undertaker' over your door?" he asked sarcastically.

"No," replied Henry "And it doesn't over yours either."

Oh," said Cuthbert, he'd been meaning to fix that.

The Captain asked if anyone had a mirror prompting Cuthbert into a lecture about vanity at a time like this.

Henry sheepishly produced a small mirror from an inside pocket and shrugged, "Old habits die hard, I always had to be ready for the cameras."

The Captain held the mirror to the lips of each 'corpse' in turn. "There," he said triumphantly "It's misted up, they're alive."

"Don't be silly," snorted Cuthbert, "They're lying on a slab, only corpses lie on slabs. I've seen it before you know," he added knowingly. He was on a roll now, so he continued, "And anyway, why does Ronald look so pale and when was the last time Percy was quiet for this long? How do you explain that?"

The Captain had been rummaging about in some semblance of a forensic search and he came up with a feathered dart, "Well this stuck in Ronald's neck wouldn't help, now would it?

Cuthbert leaned forward to examine the wound, just as something hummed overhead and the Captain sank to the ground. Cuthbert stepped to one side to catch him, just in time to hear another hum followed by Henry joining Ronald on a slab.

Aaaah, there you are Cuthbert," said a voice from the doorway, "This is WPC Hannah Cuffs..." His voice trailed off as he took in the scene before him.

"He's a serial killer," breathed the WPC, "we've caught him in the act."

"No," insisted Cuthbert, "They're all alive, look in the mirror."

"Don't try your 'all men are equally guilty psychology with us Cuthbert," hissed the Chief Inspector. "They're lying on slabs and only corpses lie on slabs."

Cuthbert shut up, he seemed to be arguing with himself.

Outside, Geraldine cursed again. After getting lost in the tunnels, she had scoured the house only to find Cuthbert in the outbuilding with witnesses, but as far as she was concerned killing a witness was all good practice. She giggled and crept away.

Chapter Nineteen

After a brief argument over who should be sat in the back with the prisoner, Cuthbert was put into the police car and delivered to PC Beeching to give them time to arrange for a convoy.

Beeching slammed the cell door and announced, "You just beat me to it there sir; you should see the dossier I've compiled on this villain.

"The WPC looked at him sceptically and purred, "Oh you must pass it on constable, it will save us hours of preparation."

Beeching spluttered, "Yes, Ma'am, Mum, Ms or Mrs." His grasp of political correctness wasn't a patch on his grasp on a pizza.

Cuthbert sat on the bench in his cell and looked around him. Percy had been in here so many times that the walls were covered in dates and cartoon drawings of PC Beeching.

Thinking about Percy, set off a train of thought, but it didn't last long enough to leave the station, so he just wondered why everyone was falling asleep.

* * *

Jasper had set up a perimeter around Cuthbert's outbuilding whilst he investigated this new mystery. After prodding Percy and kicking Ronald, he noticed the dart lying on the floor. He examined the feathers and he presumed that it had come from a Patagonian blowpipe, mostly because it said 'For size 2 blowpipe, Made in Patagonia' on the metal ferrule.

"Cecil!" he shouted and one of his 'men' stood before him quivering to attention.

Every gang had a Cecil; you had to include him because your Mum knew his Mum and you would "take him with you if you knew what was good for you."

Jasper counted to three and stabbed Cecil in the neck with the dart and then watched as he folded like a slow-motion deflating toy and a very impressed Jasper stepped over his prostrate form and left the building.

The women had been searching for their men-folk all day and the only place left was Cuthbert's outbuilding.

They weren't too keen on entering it, because of its main purpose when Cuthbert wasn't fermenting home-made wine in there.

Arkle pushed to the front after announcing that they were all a bunch of ninnies and stepped inside. After a few moments, she came back out looking rather pale, "I've found the men" she announced.

After the initial shock and the use of Henry's mirror retrieved from the floor, it was established that the men were alive, but comatose, so it was just another Sunday afternoon really.

The women couldn't carry the men, so they simply rearranged them with Henry lying with his arms crossed like the tomb of a crusader knight and the Captain and Ronald sat on a chair, each with their heads leaning together as if they were waiting for Godot.

They carried the fallen mafia member home, because his Mum would be worried.

* * *

Nobody really thought Cuthbert was a serial killer because he was too incompetent for a start; that was obvious from the way the police had caught him surrounded by bodies, but by the same token, if he was guilty, then no-one wanted to admit that he was their best friend either. Cuthbert had always been difficult to be around.

Avril, the local reporter was almost bouncing off the walls with excitement, she had warned them about Cuthbert, 'Fixation with a spiral on her notebook,' indeed.

He had been mentally weighing her and working out his recipes. Not that anyone had mentioned cannibalism of course, but nothing got in the way of a scoop, she took out her notebook.

"So how did you feel when you found out that Henry had been the victim of Cuthbert, the serial killer and cannibal?" Avril asked blocking Margery's path.

Margery paused, "Henry isn't dead and he hasn't been eaten," she explained patiently. "He's unconscious, he's stunned."

Avril changed tack, "How did you feel when Henry became a victim of the local stunner then?"

Margery found this offensive, because both she and Belinda the barmaid considered themselves to be the local stunner.

Margery reached out and gently closed Avril's notebook before saying, "Why don't you be a dear and interview the police or even Cuthbert before a real serial killer shows up?"

Avril opened her mouth ready to deliver her 'The public has the right to know' speech, but something in Margery's eyes and the very impressive grip on her notebook made her think again, so she went in search of the wife of another victim.

Elspeth had been rather enjoying quietly dusting without the Captain directing operations from his corner and when she opened the door to her visitor, it seemed a mixed blessing especially when it turned out to be Avril who dived straight in with her favourite shock tactic.

"How did it feel when you discovered that the Captain had fallen foul of the established serial killer and renowned cannibal Cuthbert?"

She watched as Elspeth hid her panic and grief by inviting her in and offering her a cup of tea.

Avril sighed, she needed to send the whole Valley on a course teaching them how to react badly to journalistic probing, or she would never get anywhere.

Elspeth watched as Avril opened her notebook and she had to admit that Cuthbert had a point. If you imagined yourself running along the shiny spiral, it would be quite an adventure.

Avril looked at Elspeth's eyes rolling and glazing over and she sighed, closed her notebook and drank her tea.

* * *

Cuthbert wasn't impressed by the service in Constable Beeching's cells; he was really missing his cup of tea and he had a farm to look after.

The policeman was nowhere to be seen and Cuthbert suspected that the mafia had stranded him somewhere again. There were only two cells and only Cuthbert's had a door on because the other one had been removed to stop Percy picking the lock.

Cuthbert traced his fingers along the walls until he found the loose brick with a picture of Percy's hat drawn on it and he took the brick out, unlocked the door with the spare key and replaced both the key and the brick.

Why Beeching should keep a spare key *inside* a cell was beyond everyone who knew about it.

Cuthbert closed the door behind him and went home.

* * *

When Constable Beeching returned, his day was really ruined. Not only had his pizza been stolen, his car had been dismantled and now his prisoner had escaped. No wonder they were building a new police station. But of course, he mused, if he could link all those disasters together…

* * *

Cuthbert entered his kitchen to the warm atmosphere of good company, fresh tea and Percy's wellies drying on the stove. "Morning all," he said.

"Morning Cuthbert," said the Captain.

"Morning Cuthbert," added Henry, still shaking from his night on the slab.

"Where have you been?" snapped Percy, "I had to make the tea."

"Oh, found the instructions did you?" asked Cuthbert sarcastically. It was good to be home.

It was still always a surprise when the door burst in and Percy was already in the room, so everyone looked up when the police entered en masse.'

The Chief Constable positioned himself on the opposite side of the table to Cuthbert to give himself some reaction time if the killer instinct should reveal itself.

WPC Hannah Cuffs was beside him and the three constables were ranged behind Percy and Ronald.

"Look," sniggered Percy, "It's handsome, handcuffs and the three stooges." He yelped as a truncheon 'slipped.'

The senior policeman intoned, "I am arresting you Cuthbert, for the murder of..."

"Who's been murdered?" Henry interrupted.

"Well, you lot," floundered The Chief Inspector.

"Do we look dead?" insisted Henry.

"*He* soon will be," giggled Hannah as another truncheon slipped and Percy yelped again.

The senior policeman turned as the door darkened and Constable Beeching sidled into the room. "That's him," He cried pointing at Cuthbert. "I was handing him a pizza for his supper when he overpowered me, stole my car and sold it for spare parts."

Percy couldn't contain himself, "When did you ever part with a pizza Constable Colossus?" This was followed by a third yelp as another truncheon 'slipped'.

Hannah had these three trained already.

The Chief Constable looked from one face to the other and he could feel his case slipping away in an avalanche of statutes and sub-sections.

"You've all been warned," he said in exasperation.

"No we haven't," said Ronald, ducking so that the accidental swing of the truncheon hit Percy.

"Yes you have," insisted the officer.

"Actually sir, they haven't" muttered the WPC beside him, "Shall I?"

Her superior nodded mutely, so WPC Cuffs put her hands behind her back and slowly circled the table causing everyone's eyes to follow her. They would have done anyway when the alternative was to look at each other.

"We need to get something straight," she began "Law and order have come to the Valley and they are here to stay. We know about the mafia, we know about fugitive mercenaries hiding out here. To put it simply gentlemen, we know where the bodies are buried."

"Wish Cuthbert did," muttered Ronald ducking again just before Percy said "Ow."

This was more than Percy could stand and he jumped to his feet startling everyone, "I don't think you know who you're dealing with here," he shouted rubbing the bumps on his head. "I could have you lot for assault by triplets I could, it was enshrined in the Magna Carta that 'All men are created equal' and that the meek shall inherit the

Earth when the equality, legality and fraternity have been run up the flagpole."

The following astonished silence was broken by Hannah shaking her head and saying, "Well the first part was the American Declaration of Independence, you twerp." Glancing around the room, she opened it to the floor with a wave of her hand.

The Captain coughed, "Well, the second part was from the Bible."

Henry contributed that "the third part was the anthem of the French revolution, but Lord knows where the flagpole came in."

The three constables raised their truncheons, but Hannah stopped them with a sigh, "It sounds as if we've done him enough damage for one day." And with wagging fingers and furrowed brows, they left.

As they drove away from Cuthbert's farm with the three constables crammed into the back seat and constable Beeching left behind on 'foot patrol,' Hannah ventured that they had certainly chosen a den of iniquity to operate in and shivered slightly as she asked how long it would take to get the police station operational.

"We'll soon see," said the Chief as he pulled in at the building site and the foreman came over to report a stolen cement mixer.

Chapter Twenty

Marvin was struggling to account for all the missing equipment and the accountants were getting more and more insistent that he come up with a rational explanation for it all; hadn't they heard of the Valley? Of course they hadn't, they never left their cosy offices and the only exercise they got was during a power cut when it was back to the abacus for everyone.

* * *

The men had decided to stretch their limbs and walk down to the Mandrake Arms and they stopped at the building site on the way to offer their expertise and advice.

Percy's solicitous, "You're not doing it like that are you?" wasn't very well received after a long and back-breaking day laying bricks, mixing cement and chasing the mafia to get the bricks and cement back to where they were supposed to be.

Percy sat on the edge of what used to be the crater and he dangled his legs over the edge. "Bet you've heard of the Statue of Liberty, eh lads? Course you have, professional builders like yourselves. One of my ancestors built that, his name was Archibald Plumm and he was commissioned especially to build the statue of a red Indian chief holding his hand up to welcome travellers to the new world on this island where they would be processed."

"That's never an Indian chief," scoffed one of the builders.

"Wait for it, wait for it" said Henry gently, as he also took a seat beside Percy.

"As I was saying" continued Percy, shuffling to get comfortable, "His job was to build this giant replica of a chief so Archibald and his team began work straight away."

The bricklayers had begun to form a crowd in front of Percy now and the questions began,

"What happened?" asked one.

"Why isn't it called the Chief of Liberty then?" asked another.

Percy held up his hand for silence and then continued, "The main problem was that my ancestor and his team had been at sea for weeks, just getting there and now they were stranded on this island within sight of the mainland and all they could think about was women.

Every time they built the chief, it had curves in all the wrong places and no matter how many times they tried, an inspection committee would come along and condemn it.

In the end, Archibald altered it just enough so that it was wearing long Grecian robes so that he could claim that the chief had just got out of the bath and the spiky crown on its head looked something like a headdress from a distance in bad weather.

The next time the committee turned up, the fog had rolled in from the sea and things looked ok, so they signed the cheque and my ancestor and his team jumped on a boat to go and spend it.

By the time the fog cleared, the committee could see the thing clearly and it was obvious that Archibald had taken a right liberty, and that gentlemen, is how it got its name."

With that, Percy jumped up and headed for the bar.

Henry paused for long enough to say, "I told you, all you have to do is wait for it."

* * *

Ronald couldn't make up his mind about this police station business, they had already referred to 'ex-mercenaries' hiding out but he was well versed in the role of 'hiding in plain sight' even though it wasn't very relaxing seeing all those police helmets and shiny buttons. He may have to disappear yet again; the obituaries were getting monotonous now.

Arkle hadn't really given the situation much thought until three identical constables had tried to bar her way on a morning cross-country ride.

Upon seeing them stood in a line side by side, she had assumed that it was a novelty event for the local gymkhana and jumped over the lot of them. Looking over her shoulder, she saw them go down like skittles and shook her head at the shoddy workmanship; the junior riders would soon wreck that event she thought.

* * *

Meanwhile, the bricklayers had cemented the new concrete mixer to the foundations and the walls were reaching ground level with individual interior walls for cells; extra cement had been used for these because even strangers could sense that it would soon become Percy's second home.

* * *

Cuthbert paused on his way to The Mandrake Arms and watched the bricks turning into walls and the walls turning into a building. He was fascinated; he had never seen anything built from scratch like this. Aunt Liza (shudder) had built the new cinema/theatre from prefabricated sections and his farm buildings had been either standing (or falling down, whichever way you looked at it) for generations.

Unfortunately, being stared at by the local undertaker did not go down well with the workmen who soon approached the foreman to tell him to clear off and measure someone else up.

Cuthbert recognised the signs because they had followed him all his life, even at school the war games were muted because no-one played dead in case his instincts kicked in and he buried them. Cuthbert sighed, waved a hand to the foreman to save him coming over and joined the others in the bar.

No-one seemed to be worried about the police presence and the conversation was lively enough as they all relaxed in each others presence.

In fact, it was so relaxed that Ronald and the Captain had fallen asleep across the table still clutching a glass each and Cuthbert leaned across to prod Ronald just to make him fall off his chair just as something hummed overhead and Henry slumped forward.

Percy had been behind the bar with Margery as she watched him tie an old sock around a leaking pipe to stop it dripping. He had heard the humming sound and he whipped off his wellies, put them on his hands and held them in front of him. Well, he reasoned, they seemed to ward everything else off, so why not this?

Margery surveyed the carnage and focused on Cuthbert, "Not again Cuthbert" she cried. "Can't you learn some new jokes or something? This is getting monotonous."

Cuthbert gaped and looked around, but there was no-one else in sight so it must be his personality again. It's a good job he preferred the quiet life.

Outside, Geraldine cursed what could only be a bent blow-pipe and wondered if she could administer the dart by hiding it in a meat pie. She slipped away quietly and returned to the museum.

Percy came out from behind the bar still holding his welly-clad hands before him and pointing them in each direction and into all the corners as if they could fire rays of whatever miasma lurked within them.

"What are you doing Percy?" asked Margery incredulously.

Percy adopted a dramatic voice and explained that there were strange forces afoot (the irony of the wellies was not lost on Margery) and he was determined to be awake and alert to combat it. Percy whipped around quickly to check another doorway causing his latest seed collection to fall out of the welly, trip him up and send him bowling down the cellar steps where he promptly knocked himself out.

Margery sighed and ignoring Cuthbert holding his empty glass went to find the real world.

Cuthbert shrugged and simply topped his glass up from all the other glasses being neglected on the table. Looking around, he realised that he could practice his conversation and his favourite anecdotes on this particularly compliant audience "Did I tell you about …?" he began.

His audience groaned in their sleep.

* * *

WPC Hannah Cuffs was quite enjoying this new posting, she would soon make everyone dependent upon her by the judicial hiding of vital paperwork and then producing it just as everyone was beginning to panic.

She sighed contentedly and leaned back in the expensive chair she had appropriated by pretending it was for her boss. It went up, it went down, it spun around and it even commanded attention when she wasn't in it.

Hannah smiled to herself; she even had Percy to torment and three malleable constables to do it with. Life was good she thought, but then another thought pushed it aside and brought a frown with it, she must make sure that her past was well hidden, *very* well hidden indeed.

Her penchant for handcuffs had begun at Madam Tootight's bondage club and the police had seemed a natural career move.

* * *

Cuthbert had staggered home after kindly finishing off everyone's drinks for them and Margery was dusting around her unconscious customers.

She stood back and muttered, "I wish I knew what was going on around here."

"You won't believe me when I tell you," said the pot plant in the corner.

Jasper was right, Margery simply refused to believe that he had seen a museum curator firing darts at her customers. What was the point, to set up a rival establishment offering rooms amongst the tombs? Playing rummy with a mummy?

The health spa in the next valley had been bad enough offering a gin and tonic with a cheap colonic, but what did Geraldine have in mind?

Jasper and Margery leant in over the table until their heads were in that close proximity where only the darkest deeds and thickest plots were formed.

* * *

Cuthbert waved cheerily to the ever-growing walls as he passed the building site, but everyone was on the other side of the brickwork.

In fact, they seemed to have concentrated on building one side so that they could hide behind it.

He continued on his way without noticing the cow fall over as he passed.

Chapter Twenty-One

Geraldine glared at the offending blow-pipe as if the heat of her hatred would straighten out any kinks in it before hitting it against a rock just to show it who was the boss.

Margery and Jasper had slipped into the Museum well after dark. No-one knew whether there were elaborate security systems in place or not, so Jasper deployed his specialist 'Cecil.'

He said to the intrepid acolyte, "Run through the building and we will listen out for any alarms."

"Yes boss," replied Cecil throwing a salute and setting off.

Margery glanced at Jasper, "You do know that I know his mum don't you?"

Jasper shrugged, "This is the mafia, who do you want to get caught, the head of the snake or its tail?"

Cecil returned breathless, but feeling useful, so Jasper sent him out to guard the perimeter and he and Margery moved forward silently.

Margery had borrowed one of Ronald's tactical suits and a balaclava; it certainly looked far better on her that it did on him.

She hadn't had the time to check the pockets or gizmos yet, but if Ronald could master, it why couldn't she?

A museum at night is a seriously spooky place and even these two hardened crime syndicate controllers stuck together as they roamed amongst the exhibits.

Egyptian eyes outlined by kohl followed them everywhere and stuffed creatures seemed to tense as they went past.

They didn't really know what to expect because no-one ever bothered to visit here in daylight and the mafia borrowed and returned exhibits when they rented them out for exhibitions, but that was in daylight when Geraldine was digging up coins planted by them as a decoy.

A sliver of light showed from beneath the door of a back room and they were drawn towards it like moths to a flame and Jasper crept closer where his young ears could relay information back to Margery.

Inside, Geraldine was muttering loudly as she looked through a catalogue for a new blowpipe and tried to figure out how to put it on museum expenses, "I'll make them pay," she said.

"She's going to charge admission," whispered Jasper.

"They'll bite off more than they can chew," Geraldine hissed.

"She's going to serve food, lots of it," relayed Jasper.

"I will be the only one benefiting," she continued.

"She's after a monopoly," supplied the mafia leader.

"They'll have to come to me, there'll be no-one else," cackled the curator.

"She's going to kill us all," gasped Jasper.

Margery stiffened and pushed past Jasper, wrenching the door open and catching one of the loops of the tactical suit on the handle as she did so.

Geraldine had a fleeting glimpse of a rather fetching apparition in overalls and a balaclava, before a blinding flash made everything seem in slow motion and the room filled with smoke.

It literally took time for the smoke to settle, but by the time it had, Jasper had scooped up any spare darts he could find and all the misunderstandings had been cleared up.

Geraldine had even made her plot to kill Cuthbert seem reasonable, although she threw the faulty blowpipe into the corner in disgust when she admitted that the 'sleeping sickness' had been due to her faulty aim.

They all had a cup of tea in mugs emblazoned with 'Archaeologists Dig It,' and then Margery gave Geraldine a hug, giving Jasper the chance to acquire the blow-pipe as well, before he and Margery made their way home.

* * *

Margery caught herself thinking about Cuthbert later when Percy staggered back up the cellar steps and she had to point him on his way to his friend's house.

What was it about Cuthbert that made people want to kill him?

Ronald had tried several times, especially when he first came to the Valley looking for Shakespeare's manuscript with Henry.

Avril had contemplated every torture devised by man or woman for him and even Arkle was on a hair-trigger with him.

Now she could understand it if it was Percy, but she had known Cuthbert all his life and he wasn't a threat to anyone.

Perhaps that was it, these outsiders brought their cynicism and phobias with them and Cuthbert made them suspicious because he didn't fit the profiles they were used to avoiding, but she had to admit that Cuthbert didn't fit any profile she had ever heard of.

Throwing a table-cloth over her gently snoring guests and patting her husband fondly on the head Margery headed upstairs.

Chapter Twenty-Two

The police car pulling up at the building site the next day didn't cause a stir of any kind now, because the workmen were used to being surrounded by uniformed men who didn't give out speeding tickets.

The Chief Inspector strolled around the site with his hands clasped behind his back and WPC Cuffs trailing along behind him, suddenly stopping to take more notice of something. He called to the foreman and he then enquired about the doors.

The foreman hesitated before explaining that he had taken the decision onto himself and installed extra wide door frames.

The Chief was impressed, "Well done that man" he said, "That's just the sort of initiative we need to make our police station all inclusive." Then, as an after thought he asked, "Are there many wheelchairs in the Valley?"

The foreman looked puzzled, "None sir, it's for Constable Beeching."

* * *

Today seemed to be full of surprises. Henry was surprised when he awoke and realised just how ravishing a tactical suit could look when Margery was inside it.

Cuthbert was surprised that Percy had come staggering in covered in bruises and Ronald was *very* surprised that his tactical suit was missing and his balaclava smelled of perfume.

Actually, the person who was the most surprised was the one who was getting the most attention.

Cecil stood stock-still as Jasper took aim and frowned in concentration as feathered missiles hummed past his target in all directions.

After a brief consultation with the mafia armourer, Jasper stuck the blow-pipe into the fork of a tree and eased against it before sighting through the tube and reloading it.

Cecil was thrilled as he could sense promotion in all this. His mum had been convinced that the mafia only wanted him for a 'fall-guy,' then the dart hit him and he did fall.

* * *

Percy was shovelling breakfast down himself like a man who had seen his friends drugged and then taken a fall down some cellar steps.

The door opened and Cuthbert moved to fill cups with tea as they were joined by Henry and the Captain.

Ronald appeared from a panel in the wall because he still didn't trust all these newcomers. The only uniforms he liked were worn by men marching in line and playing musical instruments.

Percy pushed his plate away with a sigh and said, "I hope you all saw my magnificent fighting defensive retreat manoeuvre last night. I was the only one fighting off the numerically superior forces while you lot left me to it."

Ronald nodded seriously, "I have to admit that even after all the close quarter battle courses and survival training I've had; nobody ever taught us that one Percy, I'm most impressed."

Percy stuck out his chest and prepared to elaborate, but the Captain spoke first, "It's a new one on me too Percy, according to Margery you put your wellies on your hands and fell down the cellar steps. Did they teach you that at gardening college?"

"Oh yes," guffawed Ronald, "In case of attack by truculent turnips, take immediate steps," and he started thumping the table top "And in case of assault by long orange things, give them a carroty chop."

The Captain added, "Of course lettuce can be beaten easily, it's not *rocket* science."

Percy glared at each of them in turn and decided to make a dignified exit by sliding back the panel he thought Ronald had come through and he promptly fell down Cuthbert's cellar steps. The echoing laughter followed him down the tunnels.

Chapter Twenty-Three

The Chief Inspector was pleased with his inspection; all the basement dividing walls were complete and the cells were ready for the iron doors to be fitted, this would be the most secure police station for miles, he thought.

Hearing a voice say, "Excuse me Guv," he stepped aside for a young man carrying bricks down one of the corridors. After a moment's thought, he followed and checked around the corner, there was no-one there.

* * *

Jasper had left Cecil fast asleep on his mum's doorstep for safe keeping and he called for an assembly near the building site.

Word had come down, that scaffolding had been delivered and the mafia needed to renew some of its rocket launcher tubes.

Hidden amongst the bushes, they watched as the scaffolders assembled the first level and laid boards for a walkway. They would have sprung into action as soon as the workmen had driven away, but Percy appeared and seemed intent upon checking every joint and fitting.

He really could be an obstruction when he set his mind to it, thought Jasper.

After a few whispered instructions and a single command, the mafia swarmed all over the scaffolding like pirates climbing the rigging of a captured ship.

Part of the assault involved grabbing Percy at floor level, whilst the upper level team slid a scaffold pipe down the back of his jacket, fixing him in place like a human totem pole. This allowed the teams to carry away all the poles they needed, whilst Percy squirmed and waved his arms about.

Of course, being pinioned in such a prominent place on the high street meant that a crowd soon gathered and this was swollen by the men returning from breakfast at Cuthbert's.

The comments were varied and mostly very unhelpful, "Burn him, he's a witch," cried a voice trying not to sound like Ronald.

"Firing squad prepare," called the Captain.

"Light the blue touch paper and stand back?" suggested Henry.

The women just shook their heads as Percy struggled furiously.

The men drifted away as thirst began to take precedence and anyway after Mrs Biggle had covered Percy in powder after trying to take his photograph, the entertainment seemed to have run its course.

The women began to wander off next with ever more unlikely tales of work needing to be done.

The last one involved, 'Moving all my furniture and then putting it back exactly where it was because I feng shui-ed it and there might have been an earth tremor.

This just left Margery listening as Percy pleaded, cajoled and promised free handyman services for life if Margery would only set him free.

A bush nearby whispered, "I thought one of his ancestors was an escape artist?"

Margery smiled and began to walk away, but Percy's pleading rose to a higher pitch, so she turned and sighed, "Percy, why don't you just undo the buttons on your jacket?"

Percy hesitated, tried it and said, "Oh," before he fell flat on his face.

The foreman bricklayer was able to give his lads a rest now that the scaffolders were raising a framework of poles and walkways ready for the next storey to be built and, right on schedule the electricians had arrived.

The foreman was actually quite put out by all the attention the electricians were getting, they were a preening bunch at the best of times and his men worked much harder than them, but a crowd was gathering to watch drums of cable and mysterious boxes being unloaded.

That was it he supposed, watch a bricky for ten minutes and you got the picture; mix some mud, slap some bricks on it and let it dry.

Whereas, electricity was invisible and these posers made a superb job of peeling coloured plastic back to reveal copper cores and then declaring, "Let there be light," at the end of it all.

What the foreman didn't know was that the Valley folk were extra fascinated, because there was no power supply in the Valley and he hadn't noticed, because they had a petrol-driven cement mixer.

Jasper's head electrician was full of the possibilities for the tunnels; they could string lights all along the ceilings and illuminate the campaign map in the operations room. It all seemed a bit ambitious to Jasper, because his 'Head Electrician' only acquired the post because he was tall and could reach high enough to steal a light-bulb from home and bring it here when needed. Anyway, it had been so long since the power had been on that Jasper doubted whether he could remember how to do even that simple task for them.

Percy had drawn one of the electricians to one side when they adjourned to the bar at lunch time and they were engaged in an intense discussion at a secluded table.

Gradually, the other electricians wandered over and sat down with them just in time to hear Percy claim that the most effective invention had been Alexander Graham's bell. "Think about it," He said, "They're everywhere, churches, boxing rings and there was even one on the Titanic," Percy concluded.

"Do you mean Alexander Graham Bell?" asked one of the newcomers.

"That's what I said," snapped Percy "Weren't you listening?" He continued, "You lot think you are dealing with cutting edge technology, but it all goes back to age-old mysteries, which were better forgotten."

Leaning forward confidentially, he whispered, "When the first circuit breaker was thrown and the lights came on, the people cried 'How did that happen?' and the local wise man replied 'It's witches' and they've been known as switches ever since." He leaned back, content with a job well done.

"Poppycock!" said one of the audience; swigging at his pint.

Percy studied him as he accepted a charity pint from the amused locals on the next table. "Well Mister Poppycock," he began, "You are obviously an expert in something you can't see and can't hear and yet you are happy to pay for it when for all you know, they catch the stuff free of charge."

The man spat the froth off his pint and across the table as he spluttered, "Catch it free of charge, what are you blathering about?"

Percy shook his head condescendingly, "Picture a power station," he began, and all around the table the men's eyes glazed over as they summoned the fount of all their fortunes and indeed the roots of their very existence.

"Now focus on those big, strange shaped towers you see at every one of them with steam coming out of the top."

"Cooling Towers," his audience supplied in unison.

Percy shook his head, "Lightning collectors," he stated flatly, "Alchemists and conjurors were trying for centuries to catch the lightning and the secret was the shape of the container. They tried for it at the ancient Woodhenge, but they caught fire, so they tried Stonehenge which didn't catch fire, but the lightning escaped from the gaps and that's how the Druids were wiped out."

The silence around Percy's table was complete as educated men grappled with information overload, forged by absolutely no education at all.

"In the reign of Queen Elizabeth the First, John Dee tried several methods of his own and the locals avoided the flashes and powerful rays coming from his house whenever they could, especially after the paper-lad went missing after delivering Ye Daily Parchment.

Now, John Dee tried to redirect the lightning by using mirrors to deflect it into glass jars and apparently it was working really well, until his cat knocked one of the mirrors and caused the Northern Lights."

Percy lubricated himself from another charity pint before he continued, "The only refinement the modern age has added is the shape of those towers, the lightning goes in and spins around because it can't get out again and some of it is forced down all those wires leading to the houses." He sat back again quite content as he emptied his glass.

"Balderdash!" accompanied another explosion of beer-foam across the table.

Percy sighed, "Be careful Mister Balderdash, because if I'm wrong there is only one other explanation for those towers."

The silence stretched in direct proportion to the limits of curiosity, until someone asked, "What is it?"

Percy's expression darkened, "As it warned on the ancient maps my friend, 'Here be Dragons.'"

The electricians wandered off in a daze leaving Percy with several warm pasties and bags of crisps to compensate him for his valuable time, he settled down to enjoy the lot.

* * *

The foreman back at the building site was puzzled by the change in the electricians, they seemed slightly more humble and they regarded every piece of equipment with great suspicion. This was precisely why he didn't allow his team to drink at lunchtime.

* * *

Margery cleared away the detritus from Percy's table and looked at him fondly, "Percy" she said "When you run out of words, this Valley will be a lesser place to live."

Percy's mouth opened but then his eyes widened as he looked past Margery and he suddenly made a run for the back door.

Margery watched him go as she thought, 'Be careful what you wish for girl.'

She then turned and gaped at the flame-haired female version of Percy stood in the doorway.

Even Margery's shock-absorbers had limits and she dropped her   tray.

Chapter Twenty-Four

Percy crashed into Cuthbert's kitchen gasping and wheezing, just as Elspeth, Ronald and Henry emerged from one of the tunnel entrances under Cuthbert's stairs. Cuthbert had once tried to put a chalk mark on every wainscot panel which either slid or swung open from the other side, but it looked like a giant game of noughts and crosses and he gave up and did the same thing as he did now, he put the kettle on.

Percy was gasping and pointing to himself and then indicating longer hair and a more shapely body, which Elspeth interpreted as "Percy has won a weekend Spa break."

Henry suggested, "He's asking if anyone knows whether he's dry-clean only?"

Ronald was emptying his pockets of throwing knives and lining them up. He had interpreted it as, 'Wouldn't I make a great target?'

Elspeth tried again with, "Wouldn't I make a great fashion model if fashion went out of fashion?"

All speculation ended when yet another unknown panel slid open and Margery entered. She sat down without ever taking her eyes off Percy and she even risked a sip of whatever was in the cup in front of her.

The others were just starting to worry as Margery and Percy simply couldn't break eye contact.

"Has he been at the barrels again darling?" Henry sighed.

Margery shook her head.

"Has he sold the Valley again?" growled Ronald.

Margery shook her head again.

"Parked his tractor on your flowerbeds again?" suggested Cuthbert.

"That was *him*?" flared Margery, but she still didn't look away.

"Oh come on Margery," pleaded Elspeth "This is Percy; we could be here for weeks."

Margery nodded slowly and took a deep breath before whispering,

"Percy has a sister."

* * *

Marvin had been forced to visit the building site with the road gang, the Mayor had been most insistent that there would be a regular presence whenever they could be spared, so he was in the front seat of the van whilst the drains team were in the back with the doors open to create a suction capable of pulling out all the residual fumes from yesterday's pipe blockage.

The drains inspector was driving and muttering about "Showing the flag when we could be involved in vital maintenance like de-furring the kettle."

Marvin hadn't really been listening because when he was with the road gang, he tried to keep his mouth and nose closed, so sometimes his ears closed as well.

"What flag?" he asked "I didn't know you had a flag. Why haven't *I* got a flag?" Now that he thought about it, the council had that ridiculous coat of arms showing a Mallard.

Some wag had written a motto beneath it saying, 'Give us a job and we'll duck out of it.'

The Mayor had a flag and even matching pennants on his car, so why didn't the hardest working team of them all have a flag?

Marvin allowed his imagination to freewheel; a spade crossed with a pick-axe and the acronym C.L.O.S.E.D. beneath it?

A screech of brakes and the yelps of the drains team falling out of the back interrupted his thoughts; they had arrived, he would give this matter more thought.

* * *

The silence in Cuthbert's kitchen was complete; they had never really got over the thought that Percy might have a *mother*, never mind a sister.

Percy was looking from one of them to the other and back again; even he wasn't really sure where to start with this one, but he sighed and made a start just as a car pulled up outside, but nothing could distract his audience now.

"The person you saw was my sister, Pippa."

83

"Pippa Plumm?" roared Ronald, before being shushed by Margery.

Percy continued, "She was never as accomplished as the rest of us, poor thing and she has probably got a job as a cleaner at the new police station."

The Chief Inspector entered Cuthbert's kitchen and coughed to draw reluctant attention to himself as he announced, "May I introduce you to our new commanding officer Woman Commissioner, Pippa Plumm."

The assembly gaped as an immaculately uniformed woman police officer entered with a smart white hat perched neatly on top of her red hair. With a tight smile at Ronald she said, "Put those knives away sonny, in another age, one of my ancestors would have nailed you to the mast for that." She then scanned the company, gave a brief nod to Margery and kicked Percy's stool out from under him on the way out.

WPC Hannah Cuffs wasn't at all sure about this, she was all for women's rights, but somehow, having the glass ceiling removed was one thing, but ceilings stopped the blame from falling from a great height onto those below. She could only wonder at the identity of her new superior.

Percy had picked himself up and glared at all the eyes focused on him; it was like being in a pond full of frogspawn.

Henry opened with, "So Percy, any other family failures made it to Prime Minister yet?"

Chapter Twenty-Five

Percy had stormed off to find some peace and he found himself at the dried up reservoir where he sat next to Whistle. The news couldn't possibly have travelled up here yet, but he'd forgotten that the echo system through the tunnels, together with Whistle's acute hearing all combined to feed him all of the Valley's gossip due to his hood forming a funnel to collect the sound.

"It's not just you Percy, they're everywhere these women, Whistle have to keep an eye on them; they'd try fishing, but they see us sat in the rain and think it's a bit odd. Strange chaps women."

* * *

Avril was clacking away at the old typewriter, trying to drum up some media interest in the wave of 'sleeping sickness' afflicting the Valley.

The problem was that by the time she had typed the report and posted it off, everyone had woken up; then when they fell asleep again, the same thing happened.

She glared at the expensive computer sat there enjoying its retirement, until the power lines hummed. It was quite safe because it was never long before the mafia's head electrician made a mess of removing a light-bulb only to cause a short- circuit somewhere and blow a fuse again.

* * *

WPC Hannah Cuffs straightened her blouse and tucked a loose tendril of hair back under her hat; whenever a new man took over, it always paid to make the best impression possible, so she had even padded her bra with paper towels. Every ruse greased the road to promotion, she thought.

When the door to Commissioner Plumm's office opened, the two women assessed each other immediately and each had a different reaction.

WPC Cuffs immediately noted that this was not a man who had taken over and the new boss sighed, before she said "For goodness sake woman, if you are going to pad your bra with tissues, take them out of the box first."

Hannah blushed scarlet and realised that this was not a good start and the career ladder had just become even slippier.

She also wondered why the woman behind the desk seemed so familiar, until she saw the name plaque for Woman Commissioner Plumm on the desk. Hannah Cuffs gulped.

* * *

The foreman was fascinated despite himself, when the electricians had finished the inner walls of the basement. There were different coloured wires and cables running neatly through ducting like veins and arteries, it was like being inside a great beast.

The foreman shuddered at the thought; it was too late to develop an imagination at his age, so he went to lay some bricks.

The plasterers would soon come and bury the wiring anyway.

* * *

The mafia had been delighted that the cables came on circular drums; they could roll them down the tunnels and drop the camouflaged flap back down in seconds.

The electricians had never been on a job so material intensive, it was as if the building was eating the cables.

Jasper and his men had already negotiated a sworn contract with a scrap dealer in the next valley.

He swore that he would give them a fair price for all the copper cable they brought and they swore that they would make his life a misery if he didn't.

Business was booming and the mafia account books would have looked really healthy if there had been any and if anyone could write in straight columns.

* * *

Cuthbert had served the tea and he was now trapped in the presence of a truly surreal event; Percy and Ronald were sat at his table discussing whether or not they should escape together and make a new life in another valley somewhere.

Henry and Margery had returned to the Mandrake arms so there was only Cuthbert here with them and it suddenly occurred to him that if they wanted to keep their destination a secret, they might just eliminate any witnesses.

Cuthbert made an elaborate job of stretching and yawning and announced that he was going to bed, but the two co-conspirators reminded him that it was still morning, so he sat down again.

Then he tried picking up a bucket to go and milk his cow until Percy reminded him that he didn't have one.

Then he announced that all the mice in the thatch had been very quiet and he might have to go and check on them.

"What *is* the matter with you Cuthbert?" snarled Ronald "You can come with us if you like, we'll need someone to dig up information before we settle anywhere."

"He doesn't dig things up," interrupted Percy "He's an undertaker; the clue is in the word under."

Ronald eyed Percy suspiciously and snapped, "Are you being sarcastic?"

Percy eyed him back and asked, "How would *he* know where the information was buried before we got there?"

Ronald stared and spoke very slowly, "It's an expression you ninny, like digging for gold in the hope of finding a nugget."

Percy jumped to his feet and shouted, "Oh I see, you two are leaving me behind while you go prospecting, is that the plan, is that why he's got to dig it up?"

Ronald jumped to his feet as well because he hated looking up to anyone and sitting only made it worse, "If he's the best man for the job, then the job's his." He shouted.

Percy was stunned, "So, you're getting married as well now and he's the best man, was I even invited?"

He turned his back on the pair of them and stormed out of the door.

Ronald gaped after him and turned to Cuthbert in desperation, "What just happened?" he asked.

Cuthbert shrugged, "You had a conversation with Percy, that's all" and he smiled to himself, nobody was going anywhere at this rate, he thought.

Chapter Twenty-Six

Commissioner Plumm had sent for the Chief Inspector and as he stood before her, she finished reading the crime reports for the Valley. "Are we really spending half our annual budget on combating this drivel?" she asked silkily.

The Chief Inspector tried to shrug, just to show that he hadn't believed it from the beginning, but he could recognise his signature on every page from where he stood, even when the papers were upside down. "It all came from an impeccable source Ma'am," he spluttered, "One of our front-line officers submitted the reports and the equipment lost in the riots all matches with the wreckage we found."

"Riots eh?" smiled The Commissioner, tapping a manicured nail against the reports, "One of my ancestors was a scrap dealer who bought the Titanic and he would have noticed that the only things missing from those police cars were the things which could be removed by spanners or screwdrivers. Did you check the scrap-yards Chief Inspector?"

The senior policeman blanched and his boss continued, "Is this 'front-line officer' here at the moment?"

Constable Beeching checked himself in the mirror again, he had never been interviewed by anyone this senior before; there could be only one explanation - *It was medal time.*

Commissioner Plumm looked up as the glass pane in her door darkened and a sound like a ruptured set of bagpipes came from the hallway beyond. "Come in," she called.

Constable Beeching opened the door and wriggled first one way and then the other, until he had screwed himself into the room and stood gasping before his superior.

Ms Plumm nodded to her junior officer and he placed a chair behind the constable, which promptly disappeared as he sat on it.

The Constable started to loosen his tie and gasped, "Glad I've had chance to get my breath back before the new boss comes in. Two sugars for me please, luv."

Behind him, the Chief Inspector gasped and took a step forward, but a wave of his bosses hand stopped him.

"I *am* the new boss," hissed the officer sat behind the desk.

Constable Beeching reeled from his first shock and then reeled from an immediate after-shock as the name Plumm caught his eye on the desk plaque. He made a joint decision with his wheezing lungs and decided to keep quiet.

The woman behind the desk studied the papers before her again and when she thought that Beeching may be capable of speech she asked, "How many stairs did you climb to get here Constable?"

Beeching laughed, "Hah, I get it, it's one of those promotion tests to see if I've been observant or not and have a good memory." He nodded to himself happily.

"And have you?" asked his boss.

"Have I what?" replied the Constable.

"Been observant, you've already completed the memory part" replied his superior patiently, "Do you know how many steps there are?"

"Er, no" admitted Beeching.

"The point is Constable," continued his new boss "That you were out of breath after thirteen steps and yet you claim to have pursued half the criminals in the country across half the county on foot."

Beeching concentrated on her raised eyebrow and didn't take it as a good sign, because he remembered it from school, and police college; "But they weren't running upstairs" he countered.

There was a gasp from behind him as the Chief Inspector remembered the new cabinet he'd bought to display his own medal. He would have to put books in it now. His thoughts were interrupted as his boss asked another question.

"Do you have martial arts skills, Constable Beeching?" trying to imagine him raising a leg any higher than his belt buckle.

"Er, no missus" he replied.

"And yet you single-handedly fought off the marauding hordes, who unfortunately still managed to dismantle several patrol cars entrusted to you?"

Constable Beeching hadn't been aware that the miscreants had been identified by name, but he blustered, "That's them, the Horde family, we've had trouble with them for years, the parents need a damn good talking to."

"Where are you going Chief Inspector?" hissed the Commissioner as he tried to sneak out of the room hidden by Beeching's bulk.

After that point, the duty staff that day swore that the building shook at regular intervals and that an upstairs office door was seen to bulge, only the bullet-proof glass kept it intact.

* * *

So far, the locals hadn't really given the new police station much thought, in fact they tried to not give anything much thought and they weren't even missing the post office, particularly because anything outside the Valley began to fade the longer you stayed inside it, so there was no-one to write to.

But, every time Henry wandered over to Cuthbert's farm, he found some thought trying to get his attention. He mentally rummaged through the list of jobs Margery had given him and he had successfully evaded, nope, nothing there.

Then he considered the 'hot' meat pies Jasper had been offering him at cost, but that had resulted in utter confusion because Jasper meant hot as in stolen and Henry thought they had already been microwaved, so it wasn't that either.

He politely returned a wave from the foreman bricklayer as he passed the building site and just for a second, he thought that the chap was getting really tall but with all this other stuff on his mind, he simply walked on.

* * *

Normally, when Henry entered Cuthbert's kitchen he was struck by the heat from the kitchen range and some senseless argument between Cuthbert and Percy, last time Percy had been insisting that if bodies were planted upright they would grow taller just like plants.

Cuthbert had looked at his friend in astonishment and replied, "That's ridiculous," and for a moment Henry had thought that Cuthbert was going to beat Percy's theory with the fact that the bodies were in fact, dead, but no, the undertaker had pointed out that, "I would have to dig deeper graves and the body would bang its head on the coffin when it grew."

Henry sighed at the memory and that niggling thought returned, bodies growing taller, the foreman seemed taller?

Then the heat struck him as he opened the door and he tried to decipher the latest assault on logic from this epicentre of confusion.

Ronald was holding forth about the unlikelihood of the Wooden Horse of Troy existing.

"Of course it did," snapped Percy and the Captain in a rare case of unity and the Captain pointed out the fact that it was a masterpiece of strategy and had gone down in the annals of history as such.

Ronald smiled before asking, "All right then, where did the wood come from?"

"What wood?" The newly formed duo asked.

"It was a wooden horse," explained Ronald patiently. "Troy stood between one big sandy bit and another big sandy bit; there were no indigenous trees."

Percy was puzzled now, "Indigenous? That would have made it a wooden lizard," he said.

"That's Iguana, you fool" snapped the Captain, jeopardising the new alliance, before suggesting "They dismantled one of the boats."

Ronald shook his head, "History says that the army sailed away, not 'most of them sailed away except for the ones stranded because some twerp took their boat to bits," he pointed out.

Silence descended until Percy suggested, "Perhaps it was a wooden goat, who would have taken much less wood and anyway, one of my ancestors…"

"Oh no, you don't, Percy" interrupted Ronald "Not another tall story."

Henry sat up straight; there it was again, something taller than it should have been. He shot to his feet, "That's it," he announced "That foreman is much taller than he was."

"Huh, I'll have some of that," muttered Ronald hoping there was an elixir.

Henry was still on his feet and he demanded, "Did anyone see the plans for the new police station?"

Everybody shrugged, so Henry continued, "The foreman waved to me this morning and he was at least three stories up."

"One of my ancestors was an author," began Percy.

"Not that kind of story, you twit" said an exasperated Henry. "Three storeys, three floors up, how high are they going?"

After accepting that no-one actually knew and by the time they had finished guessing, the building would be finished, Henry suggested that Marvin Middlewick was the man to ask.

"How do we get in touch with him? The Captain asked.

"I don't know," admitted Henry, "he usually suddenly appears like a genie."

Cuthbert handed him a paraffin lamp and a duster with an impossibly straight face as the others sniggered.

Chapter Twenty-Seven

Marvin Middlewick sat in his office and surveyed the pile of paperwork in front of him, he sighed.

The glory of the days when preparing the monument to the 'Fallen Heroes of the Local Authority' had long gone and the C.L.O.S.E.D. plaque on his desk no longer fooled anyone.

This load of work came from the archives and he gave it a tentative poke with his finger, hoping it would turn to dust, but it didn't.

Marvin was slightly startled when his intercom crackled into life, but either his shared secretary was eating crisps, or she'd spilled coffee into the microphone again. "Send him in," he said resignedly, the novelty of a surprise visitor was too good to miss.

Marvin stared as Henry, Percy, Ronald, the Captain and even Cuthbert entered his office and stood around shaking slightly.

Marvin tried to put them at ease with "Oh come on gentlemen," he said without including Percy in his sweeping glance, "I know that the Local Authority can seem daunting to outsiders, but you all seem quite shaken."

Henry explained that it was an emergency and they had travelled over on Percy's tractor, but the vibrations should settle down soon.

Marvin listened carefully and maintained a calm exterior, but inside his emotions were churning, contravening local bye-laws, lack of planning permission and damaging the architectural integrity of the high street.

Oh he liked that last one, he could scent a new crusade and his in-tray would soon be filled with crosswords again.

He assured his visitors that he would bring the full weight of the Local Authority to bear upon this matter.

He picked up the phone and asked to be put through to Commissioner Plumm.

As he waited, he contemplated the name Plumm, unusual name that, he thought, two Plumms in one Valley eh, they would soon be a punnet.

His smile slipped slightly as he was forced to make an appointment to see the senior police officer, but he tailored his conversation so that he sounded dominant in front of his audience, even though they could hear the purring sound as the other end put the phone down.

After his visitors left, he alerted the Mayor to this new crisis and sent for urgent copies of plans and blueprints from that strange subterranean office where the staff never saw daylight and laid large sheets of paper out on huge tables as if they were plotting the Battle of Britain.

* * *

Woman Commissioner Plumm looked up as her door opened and several people carrying rolled up sheets of paper entered her office and lined up before her, completely filling the available space.

Focusing on the person slightly in front of the others who wasn't carrying anything, she used her deductive powers and asked, "Marvin?"

He nodded, pleased that his superior standing had been noted.

The Commissioner then said, "And this I presume is the whole population of the village of Middlewick?"

Marvin glanced around and spluttered, "These are representatives of the various departments concerned and ready to combat the blatant infringements to the architectural integrity of the village high street."

Ms Plumm tapped her fingernail and raised that 'early-warning-eyebrow' as she spoke, "Do you realise that you are blocking my exit and that is 'obstructing an officer,' and that if you do not move when I try to reach the door, that will be 'Impeding an officer in the course of her duties,' and if I have to battle my way to the door, you will all be 'Injured by an officer, going about her lawful enjoyment of the use of pepper spray?"

Marvin sensed the door open quietly behind him and he instinctively knew that he was suddenly alone, he gulped.

"Now then," purred the woman he had come to berate, "What can I do for the same Local Authority which helped to cut my budget for riot shields last year?"

Marvin was suddenly less sure of the strength of his official standing, but the fact that there was not a chair for visitors, certainly *left* him standing.

After an intense discussion, during which the only thing to get heated was the coffee Marvin wasn't offered, he left the building, only to find that his colleagues had left all the plans and blueprints wrapped in cardboard tubes in the police station foyer and they had been blown up as 'suspicious items.'

He sighed and returned to *his* world, where everyone knew their place and the public paid for it.

* * *

The men were now quizzing the electricians and the bricklayers, "You must know what the plans are," said Henry, but again shrugs seemed to be the main method of communication.

According to the foreman, every time a new platform appeared on the scaffolding, they added more layers of bricks and the electricians confided that, "Once it was finished, they had to build a huge radio mast on top, so that the patrol cars could communicate with each other."

Margery and Jasper had been listening and it still didn't seem to be a problem, because the mafia still had the tunnels as their natural 'rat-runs,' completely out of sight, so business would still go on in all weathers.

Jasper's main problem at the moment was the fact that the walls for the basement had blocked his camouflaged tarpaulin access into the tunnels and made it difficult to remove items. He wondered whether the foreman would be renting a crane at some stage, because that would make life very interesting indeed.

* * *

The Chief Inspector sat alone in his office cursing Beeching and his own short-sightedness; that was the trouble with police work, the men on the ground could have all the fun from a transport café car park, shouting into their radios and banging two planks together, while someone else shouted, "Look out, he's got a gun" and all the time they were really sharing out bacon sandwiches.

By the time the reports had been filed, everyone had disappeared somewhere into the labyrinth of the shift system and no-one could read the signatures. In fact, the only time the signatures were legible was on the overtime claims forms.

He sighed and unlocked the bottom drawer in his desk, taking out a magazine, he sighed again as he studied his first love, the theatre. If early retirement was really as close as Woman Commissioner Plumm had indicated, then he had better prepare to re-invent himself and who was better at re-invention than an actor?

Chapter Twenty-Eight

Cuthbert stood alone on the stage in the 'new' theatre; it still didn't have the atmosphere of the old one and it just wasn't the same without the tractor seat in the front row.

The new Chief Inspector had prompted Cuthbert to wonder about staging another play to take everyone's minds off whatever was bothering them.

He wasn't sure what it was because he hadn't really been listening, but the fact that Percy had a sister and she was going to run the new cop-shop was going to take some beating, even the Bard might struggle to eclipse that one.

* * *

Avril had been watching the building rise phoenix-like out of the crater of Mrs Biggle's post office and she had high hopes for a stream of exclusives from this new woman Commissioner; some wag had tried to convince her that it was Percy's sister, yes she'd fallen for some tricks and tales in the past, but really, how dumb did they think she was?

It was not only the building that Avril had been watching, she had seen Geraldine acting strangely for a while now, then she had disappeared from view and now she was sneaking about again.

Avril took out her notebook and left the office, it felt good to be back in the world of scoops and potential bye-lines again. She set off to where she had last seen Geraldine.

* * *

The Commissioner studied the three constables stood rigidly before her and sighed, it was like being a totem-pole inspector, she had the sudden urge to pull one of the truncheons sharply downwards to see if she had won the jackpot. Struggling with the image of a shower of golden tokens pouring from one of the constables' mouths, she turned her back on them and regained her usual demeanour, before facing them again.

"All right gentlemen," she began "You've been here for a while, where do you think the problems lie?"

The left-hand Constable replied promptly, "The mafia Ma'am."

The central Constable added, "The mercenary, Ronald Ma'am."

The right-hand Constable had been out-manoeuvred and he was forced to say, "Percy Plumm Ma'am" trying to stop his eyes from being dragged to the desk plaque as if it was an optical magnet.

Woman Commissioner Plumm nodded slowly before saying, "Good work men; astute observations. One of my ancestors was young once, he would have been proud of you. Get back out there and catch your men. "Or," she addressed the right-hand constable "In your case, Percy."

The constables hitched a ride on the next builders supply truck to the Valley, hanging onto the sides like their comedy predecessors, The Keystone Cops.

They were on a mission and they had official sanction, although the left-hand Constable was a touch nervous as he seemed to have volunteered to arrest the mafia.

The centre-constable also had some misgivings about tackling Ronald with his reputation for world-wide mayhem.

Perhaps it was time to cause some confusion and rearrange them-selves, in the chaos; the right-hand constable would never suspect his own colleagues.

Chapter Twenty-Nine

Geraldine peered around yet another corner, where was everybody?

Her new blow-pipe had been delivered along with a new set of darts, but it was longer than the old one, so she was using it as a walking stick to disguise it.

Geraldine paused, there was Percy. It was heaven sent; he had stepped out of the Mandrake Arms and paused to study something he had taken from his pocket. He was stock-still, the perfect target. Geraldine slid a dart into the pipe, sighted along its length and blew. Her cheeks bulged, her eyes bulged and even the blow-pipe bulged as the mud lodged in the end caused the dart to shoot back into Geraldine's throat.

Both Percy and Avril dashed to her aid when they saw the museum curator choking.

Percy slapped her on the back and the dart shot out only to lodge in Avril's neck.

Avril's eyes widened in surprise as she plucked the dart out and looked at it, just before she collapsed like a bag of turnips.

Percy looked at Avril, then he looked at Geraldine and then he looked at the dart and then he ran.

Behind him, Geraldine cursed and tried to poke the end of the tube clear, so that she would get a clear shot at him; her brain was screaming "No witnesses." But Percy was gone.

* * *

Percy crashed dramatically into Cuthbert's kitchen and then did it again when no-one heard him, then he crashed into each of Cuthbert's outbuildings, but the drama was decreasing and his shoulder hurt. Eventually, he found Cuthbert in the theatre, but it was a huge space and there were no doors nearby.

"Geraldine, Geraldine," he babbled pointing at himself and simulating collapse.

Cuthbert smiled knowingly, "Yes mate, she can have that effect; I fell for her once."

Percy gave up and waited until his breath came back and his heart stopped hammering against his ribs. When he explained, Cuthbert remembered the sound in the Mandrake Arms just before everyone fell asleep.

"Did it make a humming sound?" Cuthbert asked excitedly.

"What sort of humming sound?" Percy asked, frowning.

Cuthbert demonstrated "Hummmmm."

Percy rocked his hand to say, 'Maybe, but not quite.'

Cuthbert tried again, but before he could start, they both heard a 'hum' pass between them.

"That's it, "said Percy, "perfect that time mate." Then he followed Cuthbert's gaze and saw Geraldine coming towards them. They both ran.

Bursting out of the back entrance, Cuthbert and Percy almost ran into Arkle exercising her horse and her roar followed them as they headed for the hills.

Next out of the door came Geraldine very close to being out of breath and clutching a blow-pipe.

Arkle took in the scene immediately and her hunting instincts kicked in, the mathematics were simple, two running weasels = prey, "Tally-Ho," she shouted grabbing Geraldine and seating the curator behind her, the horse responded in the way it always did to Arkle's prompting and took off like the wind.

Geraldine had the perfect stable platform to aim from by resting the pipe on each of Arkle's shoulders in turn, depending which way Cuthbert and Percy jinked.

Hooves thundered, darts hummed and the ground shook as the quarry desperately tried to go to ground.

Henry and the Captain stood on the high ground and watched the scene below, Henry smiled fondly at his daughter, "Kids" he said "They never grow up do they?"

The three constables were going to spread out and hunt for their targets individually, but the left-hand constable couldn't bring himself to enter the tunnels alone in search of the mafia and the centre-constable was imagining Ronald behind every bush, when in fact it was the mafia *inside* every bush and Ronald was in the tunnels.

As for Percy, they were all in denial at the fact that he had just run past them screaming for help and was being pursued by a two headed mound of tweed on horseback firing darts at him.

Cuthbert on the other hand knew where the bodies were buried and of course, where they were not, so he dived into an open grave and tried to remember where he had put the body this time as the earth shook and fresh soil cascaded around him as the pursuit passed by very close to the edge of his hideout.

The newcomers like Henry, Ronald, Arkle, the Captain and his wife Elspeth had realised early on that time in the Valley didn't pass at the same rate as it did anywhere else.

The locals didn't notice because it was just a fact of life to them, it was either time to get up or time to go to bed or time to go to the pub or time to go home, why complicate it?

But with a solid structure like the police station appearing to grow on a daily basis, it reflected badly on the residents if they should happen to wonder what they had achieved in the same time.

The obvious solution was to not consider the thought at all and that saved even more time.

Chapter Thirty

Henry and Ronald stood watching the builders; there were now roofers, plasterers, electricians and the original bricklayers.

They had tried to establish a hierarchy, so that one team could feel superior to the others, but the brickies and plasterers tended to feel inadequate anyway because they actually got their hands dirty and the plasterers in particular, could soon be accused of simply smearing mud on the walls.

The electricians had always considered themselves to be the elite because they stayed clean and everyone relied upon them to light up the dark corners and provide somewhere to put the kettle on. But the roofers had the best claim to justify their aloofness because simply by the nature of putting the lid on a building, they looked down on *everyone*.

At least now, Henry could see how high the building was going to be; it was three storeys tall and then the radio mast had to be added. It wasn't a pretty building, by any means and it blocked the view of the hills.

Henry could sense the start of a crusade; he would start a protest group and call it 'Citizens Opposed to the Police Station.'

He called the first meeting to order in the Mandrake Arms that evening and as a courtesy, he had invited Woman Commissioner, Pippa Plumm, the Chief Inspector and WPC Hannah Cuffs to attend.

Margery made sure that everyone had been sold a drink and nodded to Henry to begin.

Henry used his dulcet ex-newscaster voice to maximum effect as he outlined his fears for the heritage of the Valley and the future of its children, ignoring a snort from the pot plant in the corner. At the end of his speech, Henry lowered his voice to add extra gravitas and finished off with, "And this is the reason I am establishing Citizens Opposed to the Police Station. He bowed slightly to acknowledge a smattering of applause and sat down.

Commissioner Plumm stood up slowly and thanked Henry for including them in the consultation, even though, she pointed out that "it sounded more like an ultimatum."

Henry was determined, "You will not deflect me from my path" he insisted and folded his arms just to show how resolute he could be.

Ms Plumm smiled and asked, "What was the acronym for this pressure group of yours again, Mister Chisolm?"

Henry's lips moved silently as he ran the title through his mind before triumphantly announcing "C.O.P.S."

"But Henry," teased the officer, "Aren't *we* the cops?"

Margery cringed, she had seen this one coming, but she could only watch as her husband spluttered, "Err, well, yes but..."

The Commissioner's voice hardened as she pointed out that, "Anyone else masquerading as a cop could be seen as 'Impersonating an officer' and we wouldn't want that now would we?"

Henry's shoulders sagged as Ms Plumm continued, "In fact, most of my ancestors were policemen, one of them developed an early warning system in a tall tree to keep an eye out for Vikings; he had a special branch." She smiled at Henry, the way a snake would smile if it had lips and stood up to lead her entourage out.

Henry shook his head as he watched the officers take their leave. After they had gone, he turned to Margery and asked plaintively, "Why don't we ever achieve anything in this Valley darling?"

Margery patted his hand sympathetically and whispered, "Probably because the women don't handle it dear."

Ronald had stepped into the shadows when the police came and went; they had stood and discussed the new building before driving away. The ex-mercenary now stepped back into the open as the Captain came level with him. They nodded to each other in a very masculine way to show that they both had military backgrounds and the Captain asked what he was doing.

"Just making plans," said Ronald vaguely before shouting, "Oi, shorty, front and centre, right now" to a nearby bush.

A sullen member of the mafia detached himself from the foliage and glared at him.

"How did you know he was there?" asked the Captain rather impressed.

Ronald shrugged, "They're never far away" and he addressed the youth again, "Fetch Jasper and be quick about it."

A bush behind Ronald sneered, "For an ex-soldier you're not very good at the 'Hearts and minds' side of things are you?" and Jasper stepped out into view.

Ronald shrugged, "I've got no heart and I don't mind, pretty much covers it doesn't it?"

Everyone could tell that Ronald was distracted as he stared at the building standing quietly before them; it seemed to sleep until the workmen swarmed all over it again the next day. Ronald seemed to rouse himself, "Right, Jasper," he began "I need the box of specialised bugging equipment from the secret compartment in my room, I'll tell you how to find it."

"You mean this one?" asked Jasper placing a box on the floor between them.

Ronald tried to hide his amazement by saying, "And the specialised tool kit cunningly disguised as kitchen implements."

"Ok," said Jasper as another box joined the first one.

Ronald gritted his teeth and growled, "There is also a transmitter disguised as ultra-violet fly killer."

"Really?" asked Jasper in shocked surprise.

"Hah," shouted Ronald, "Beat you at last."

"Just kidding," Jasper replied as another box joined the pile.

The next few hours were incredibly instructive as the mafia taught Ronald and the Captain all they knew about secret bugging devices and the installation of such items.

Ronald went from scepticism and sarcasm to taking notes, as microphones were hidden behind power-points and ventilation ducts and the fly-killer was installed in the canteen where anything worth listening to would be said.

Everything was battery powered and the signal was beamed to Ronald's room in the Mandrake Arms, or so he thought.

The mafia had installed a separate transmitter beaming a signal to their headquarters in the tunnels and there was a time delay on Ronald's, so that the mafia could intercept all messages and block anyone else hearing anything too sensitive. They hadn't quite taught Ronald, *all* they knew.

Chapter Thirty-One

Cuthbert and Percy were in a state of high alert, they had made it back to Cuthbert's farm, but Arkle and Geraldine were still out there; it was like being hunted by a centaur dressed in tweed and smelling of horse.

The workmen had entered that welcome phase where the roof was on the building and they could work on it and stay dry.

If only the electricians would get a move on, they could have a cuppa. The electricians were actually only just realising how big a job this was, there was a huge amount of state of the art equipment being unloaded and stored in the basement and they would never admit it, but a lot of it was a bit advanced for them.

The Chief Inspector looked into his cup and realised why visiting police officers never accepted a drink from the public.

Whatever this was, he had stirred it and the moment he stopped, it had started to creep back in the opposite direction.

Pushing the cup away discreetly, he broached the reason for his visit. It was hard work because both Cuthbert and this Percy chap seemed incredibly distracted; he tried to drum up some enthusiasm with, "We could stage The Merchant of Venice, plenty of sumptuous costumes for the ladies and some good meaty roles."

He giggled at his own pun with reference to the pound of flesh demanded by Shylock, but his kitchen audience were unmoved.

When one of them was watching the front door, the other one seemed to be watching what appeared to be a tunnel entrance behind the longcase clock.

After a while, he gave up and interrupted all the furtive glances and nervous starts at the slightest noise by demanding to know what was going on. He soon wished that he hadn't bothered.

Apparently, they were being hunted by some mythical beast which had obviously been magnified by some over imagining.

At first it had been 'Arkleonahorse,' whatever that was, but then they had refined it into a centaur with two heads and shooting flaming arrows at them.

As if that wasn't enough, Percy had suddenly realised that if it entered the tunnels, it must be a Minotaur, because that's where Minotaurs lived.

The policeman slammed his hand down on the table before these two could demand being rescued by Jason and the Argonauts and he wondered why they were looking over his shoulder and whatever was that humming noise?

Standing up suddenly to assert his authority, he blocked Geraldine's view completely and felt a stab in his neck before falling across the table.

Cuthbert and Percy ran for the tunnels.

* * *

Ronald was stood on the High Street chatting to the Captain and oblivious to Jasper, picking his pocket when Percy burst through he camouflaged tarpaulin flap, collided with the outer basement wall and hurtled through the village, wailing as if bailiffs were trying to reclaim his wellies.

"Whatever is wrong with that strange little chap now?" asked the Captain.

Ronald shrugged, "I reckon that when God issued heads, Percy thought he said beds and asked for a big soft one."

* * *

Margery had been watching as Jasper had bugged the new police station, most of the wires and devices would disappear under fresh plaster and behind fittings now and no-one would ever know they were there. Margery smiled, all law abiding citizens should welcome a police presence in their town, but only if they could have inside knowledge to give them a chance to *stay* law abiding.

* * *

Whistle had honed his patience over the years in his constant battle against those elusive denizens of the deep, but he was really startled when Cuthbert defied gravity and sat gasping beside him. He turned his hood slightly and said, "If we keep meeting like this Cuthbert, Whistle need another rod."

* * *

Avril couldn't quite account for part of her day and the side of her neck was sore, but she had found her way back to the office and saw the notes scribbled on her spare notebook on the desk. "That's it," she said, failing to snap her fingers, "I've had the sleeping sickness, I can write a first hand account after I've warned the others."

Grabbing her bag, she dashed into the street again and shouted to a familiar but shadowy figure just behind Percy.

"Geraldine!" shouted Avril "Call a meeting in the..." the sentence was never completed as Geraldine instinctively whipped around and fired a dart at this newly perceived threat.

Avril crumpled, Geraldine cursed and Percy ran.

* * *

The Captain and Ronald had joined Henry in the bar and they were swapping tales of darkest Africa; the Captain had told how he had advised a safari group to climb the nearest and tallest tree if the lions began moving towards them, but an old lady had sniffed and insisted that she was too old to climb a tree.

"Madam," the Captain had said, "If the lions charge I promise that you will be reborn and you *will* climb that tree.

This was also Elspeth's territory, because as a woman she had been condescended to all over the world and when she was a guide on the same safari, she had offered different advice when a man asked what to do if the lions came at them.

"Stand still until they lose interest in you and they'll wander off." Elspeth had advised.

"But what if they don't lose interest and they keep coming?" gasped the man."

Elspeth had elaborated and explained that he must "Back off slowly and if they still keep coming, throw dung at them."

The man was panicking now, "What if there is no dung?"

Elspeth was able to reassure him that "There would be, I can guarantee that."

Percy ran until his wellies were cycling in thin air, this could only mean one thing "Uh-oh" he said as fell into a hidden entrance to the tunnels.

* * *

The three constables stood rigidly with their backs to each other and knuckles aching from gripping their truncheons over a long period. T

They had been led into the tunnels whilst chasing the mafia and they were struggling with the concept of having no night vision and each of them possessing a completely different sense of direction.

The constables managed to huddle together and edge towards the scuffling noise ahead in the darkness hoping it wasn't the thundering, dart firing juggernaut which had been the real reason for running into the tunnels.

The mafia had just been a convenient excuse.

* * *

Woman Commissioner Plumm was slightly concerned at the lack of reports from the three constables, she suddenly remembered from her school history class that when the Romans had come to Britain, they had named a tribe Dumnonii or 'Deep Valley dwellers.' It could well have been this bunch she thought, especially with the emphasis on the 'dumb.'

* * *

Percy stood up and brushed himself down and stared intently into the dark tunnel where the furtive steps were coming from. It didn't sound like the council drains team and he certainly recognised the slap of his own wellies, so he lowered his voice and intoned, "Who dares disturb me in the tunnels of my ancestors?"

The three constables stopped dead and one of them whispered "Whose that?" to his companions who shrugged in the dark to absolutely no effect at all because he couldn't see them.

"I asked you first," pointed out the strange voice.

The constables assumed an official stance at attention which was just another pointless gesture in the dark and they began to speak.

The left-hand constable quickly prodded the other two to check that he was indeed on the left-hand side; he didn't want to speak out of turn.

Satisfied that they would all be conducting themselves in an orderly manner, the left-hand constable said, "We are Her Majesty's representatives of the law."

The centre-constable added, "And we are here to uphold it."

The right-hand constable finished with "At all costs."

The mystery voice seemed impressed as it asked, "Hmm, do you carry a badge?"

The left-hand constable paused, "No, we have a warrant card."

The centre-constable added "In a wallet."

The right-hand constable added proudly, "A plastic one."

The voice previously known as Percy sneered, "A plastic wallet with a card in it, Her Majesty seems a bit of a cheapskate."

The constables drew in a collective breath at this and the truncheons creaked at the extra pressure being applied.

Percy continued, "Don't you get to wear one of those shiny pointy stars then?"

He could sense the three heads swivelling in the dark trying to look at each other in amazement.

The left-hand constable spluttered, "That's a sheriff"

The centre one added, "Or a Marshall."

The right-hand constable finished with, "We don't have one of those."

"Nottingham did," insisted Percy casually.

The left-hand constable asked, "Did what?"

"Had a Sheriff," said Percy "That's why they called him the Sheriff of Nottingham."

The left-hand constable insisted, "Well, we don't have one."

The centre constable asked, "Is that because the Queen can't afford one then?"

The right-hand constable gasped, "You can't say that, it's against one of those old laws that I can't pronounce, take it back."

The centre constable insisted, "It's a free country; I can say what I like."

The left-hand constable joined in with, "We're the Police; you know it's *not* a free country, now stop speaking out of turn."

This was followed by a 'Bonk' as if a truncheon had 'accidentally' struck someone's helmet, as someone else insisted that it "wasn't him who spoke out of turn, it was one of the others who stood in the wrong place."

This was followed by more 'bonks' until the left-hand constable tried to restore order. "Stand shoulder to shoulder," he shouted "and charge this miscreant cloaked in darkness-charge!"

Percy stepped back into a junction in the tunnel as he felt the rush of air caused by three irate constables charging past him and heading even deeper into the darkness. He decided to explore this new tunnel of opportunity and he set off accompanied by the steady slap of his wellies.

* * *

Arkle had carried Avril back to her office and settled her comfortably in her chair. Whilst this seemed the charitable thing to do, it caused utter confusion to the reporter when she awoke.

She distinctly remembered shouting to Geraldine to warn her of something, but something else had intercepted her and she had been transported here. She gasped, was there a bigger story here, could it be the only story the weekend papers were prepared to buy? Had she stumbled upon the alien abduction story of all time? She imagined the headline, 'Ace Reporter Almost Abducted. Aliens Scared Off by the Power of the Press.'

Avril's fingers flew, perhaps this is why she had been sent to this news-forsaken spot, perhaps her editors had really seen her potential and ignoring her had been part of the ruse to lure the aliens in?

She typed like a demon until Arkle stuck her head around the door, "Ahh you're awake" she said, I nearly laid you out on the desk but I didn't want you to wake up with Cuthbert measuring you, so I put you in the chair because you're a bit of a wuss."

Avril stared at the piles of paper covered in her dramatic prose before her and screwed every one of them into a tight ball before launching it at the bin. Then suddenly she was on her knees scrabbling to straighten all the paper out, "What if Arkle is the alien?" she muttered, knowing that if she was right, the world was already lost.

Chapter Thirty-Two

The police station now had a roof and the cables were all laid vertically and horizontally in neat stretches of trunking ready for the plasterers to bury it all and leave a nice smooth finish for the painters who would cover the lot in some institutional two-tone green so that everyone visiting would be in no doubt that this was a Government building right at the end of the colour spectrum of officialdom.

The control room was another matter though, the consoles had been screwed to the floor and the screens were installed, but there were still multi-coloured cables bursting out and dangling as if some electronic beast had been ritually disembowelled.

The electricians were on the verge of sending for help at the end of that particular shift, but were too embarrassed to mention it because the unspoken 'code of the sparky' demanded that 'No-one shall ever be judged superior to the electrical installations engineer and he shall uphold the tradition of always going home with his hands cleaner than when he arrived.'

So you can imagine the relief the next day when they arrived and the installation was complete, the boss must have sent specialists in during the night.

Jasper and his men were resting contentedly back at their headquarters. They had worked all night to complete the installation of the control room whilst at the same time upgrading their own surveillance screens and running cables through the tunnels so that whatever the police saw, the mafia saw and whatever the police heard or said, the mafia acted upon.

Jasper sighed contentedly. As soon as the power came on all the screens would flicker into life and this place would be like Cape Canaveral.

* * *

The three constables could see a patch of light up ahead and they staggered uphill until a fisherman sat above them could point in the direction they needed to take.

113

After thanking him and staggering on again, they began to discuss things.

The left-hand constable said, "There was no bait on that fisherman's hook."

The centre-constable added, "He didn't have a keep-net for his catch either."

The right-hand constable snapped, "Hardly relevant though is it? There was no water."

They left the tunnels and stepped out onto what appeared to be a concrete lake, but after all this time they had spent in the Valley, it didn't even raise a comment.

* * *

Cuthbert was in his outbuilding; it was always the best place to be when he was hiding, because even people looking for him hesitated when they saw a long forgotten body propped up in there, so it was a surprise when he turned and saw three dishevelled constables watching him intently.

Cuthbert had been washing his slab down after crushing tons of raspberries for his home-made wine and the juice had smeared everywhere.

The left-hand constable asked, "What's going on here?" nodding towards the slab.

The centre constable said, "And there" nodding to the floor.

The right-hand constable gulped and stared at a shrouded shape propped up behind the door, "And especially there" he said.

Cuthbert looked at each of the constables and then at the scenes of his 'crimes,' and simply held his hands out in front of him. He'd been here before.

* * *

Jasper had faced many trials and challenges in the Valley, but this new one was coming from an unexpected source.

He had noticed on several occasions that some of his men were covered in a white powder and after quizzing them, it turned out that Mrs Biggle was becoming very curious about the mafia and its methods and every time she had watched them doing something, she had tried to 'Google' it on her powder compact to see if they were doing it right.

The worrying thing was that her enquiries always involved explosives.

Hiding himself behind the pot plant in the Mandrake Arms, he overheard Mrs Biggle pleading with Margery to help her to "blow the top bit off the new police station, so that she could have her post office back." Margery had assured her that everyone was keeping an eye on things and if it was at all possible she would be back in business soon. Mrs Biggle left and Margery raised an eyebrow at the pot plant which made a note to check its inventory regularly.

Chapter Thirty-Three

Cuthbert sat on a hard chair at a table in the interview room as the three constables sat opposite and quizzed him. It seemed to be the standard 'good-cop on the left, bad cop in the middle and confused cop on the right' routine.

It was further complicated by the workmen going in and out constantly, because this was where they stored any boxes whose labels had dropped off, so they had to open them at random and at regular intervals.

The left-hand constable asked, "What were you doing in there Cuthbert?"

"The centre constable insisted, "We know what you were doing Cuthbert."

The right-hand constable asked, "So why are we asking?"

Cuthbert looked from one to the other and looked away every time a workman stepped over his feet muttering, "Ooops, sorry mate" and again when he dropped a box on either his or a constable's head.

Cuthbert really didn't stand a chance as the questions and apologies reached fever-pitch.

Left-hand constable: "What were you doing Cuthbert?"

Electrician: "Ooops, sorry mate."

Centre-constable: "We *know* what you were doing, ouch that hurt."

Plumber: "Sorry Guv, heavy box."

Right-hand constable: "How do we know what; get that bag off my foot."

"Huh," said the plasterer "You're in our store room," whilst heaving the heavy bag onto his shoulder, so that the split-end leaked pink powder over all the constables.

It looked like the result of asking Mrs Biggle to ring for help.

Cuthbert wasn't at all sure why he was here and it wasn't even as if Percy was involved this time.

He looked around as the constables were trying to clear the powder from their eyes and he simply stood up, walked across the room and hid in an empty box. The gasps of amazement still reached him as the constables looked around.

"He's gone," said the left-hand constable.

"He can't have," insisted the centre constable.

The right–hand constable swung his truncheon experimentally at the space where Cuthbert had been, there was no 'bonk!' "He has you know."

The constables dashed about trying to seal the building, but there were workmen coming and going everywhere.

They were just about to send for a helicopter when a police car pulled up and Police Commissioner Plumm and WPC Cuffs stepped out.

The Commissioner stared at her constables as they shuffled into formation and stood to attention with truncheons presented. The intentions were good, but the tear-streaked powder on all their faces and the torn uniforms and flapping epaulets from the tunnel adventure rather spoiled it all.

Ms Plumm shook her head as she inspected the rank, "Did you lot really finish first in your class or did you *finish first* and leave the others to complete it properly?"

WPC Hannah Cuffs giggled quietly in the background.

The left-hand constable spoke, "Arrested master criminal Ma'am."

The centre constable added "Arrested, past tense Ma'am."

The right-hand constable finished with "'Cos he's gone now Ma'am."

The constables and the WPC followed The Commissioner upstairs to the interview/store room where Cuthbert was sitting patiently at the table.

The constables emitted a range of sighs, grunts, gasps and threatening movements, but the Commissioner waved them to silence and listened patiently as they explained how they had lost Percy the mass-twerp, but apprehended Cuthbert the mass-murderer (again).

The decision was made to examine the crime scene, so Cuthbert was placed in the back of the police car with Ms Plumm driving and Hannah in the front, whilst the constables ran behind.

It took almost superhuman discipline on the part of the Commissioner to not keep speeding up and slowing down, but she controlled herself and they arrived at Cuthbert's farm.

At the back of The Commissioner's mind, was the fact that her Chief Inspector was missing, so she could only hope that these clods had preserved the crime-scene the way they had been taught.

She entered the outbuilding and almost cried; the slab was covered in what could possibly be blood, but there were finger-marks smeared in it where the three clods had slipped on their own muddy footprints from the tunnels and steadied themselves.

The crime-scene was a shambles, there was no tape across the doorway and no-one had been left on guard.

Ms Plumm looked forlornly around at the interior, noting the tarpaulins tied together with string behind the door and the wine-making fermentation jars on a shelf. There were also empty fruit boxes strewn on the floor in a corner.

"See Ma'am, over there," gasped the left-hand constable.

"And under there," wheezed the centre constable.

"It's behind you," giggled the oxygen starved right-hand constable.

Just at that moment, a drowsy Chief Inspector staggered into the room confirming Ms Plumm's sudden reservations about what she was seeing.

Maintaining eye contact with Cuthbert, she dragged her fingers through the mess on his slab *and licked them*.

The three constables felt their stomachs lurch; this was taking forensics too far for their liking.

"Yum," said the Commissioner, "Raspberry Cuthbert?" somehow she made it sound like a dessert.

Cuthbert nodded at that and then nodded again when she suggested that he "put the kettle on."

As Cuthbert walked across his farmyard, the outbuilding seemed to explode with sound, he caught "Wine-making" and "tarpaulins rolled up," but the rest must have been police jargon, so he just went on his way.

When Cuthbert entered his kitchen, he already had a reception committee waiting and he was touched that everyone was so concerned about him until Ronald explained that Percy was convinced that Cuthbert would get twenty years and this was a 'meet the new owner' coffee morning.

Percy slinked out of Cuthbert's usual seat and sat scowling into his wellies.

Commissioner Plumm actually betrayed her surprise when she came into Cuthbert's kitchen and joined them, but just as she was about to ask how they had all crossed the farmyard without her officers seeing them, a panel slid back and Elspeth entered sheepishly to take her seat and Ms Plumm said, "Oh."

Percy's eyes had widened and his 'fight or flight' reactions were primed at the sight of his sister. He tipped his hat forward and adopted his best Humphrey Bogart drawl as he said, "Of all the bars in all the world…"

"You had to hit me with the iron one, "snapped his sister, stealing his thunder completely. The siblings glared at each other and Pippa Plumm snarled, "So, this is where the family loser has been hiding. What alibi have you given these poor souls for your presence amongst them?"

Percy sat up straight to defend himself, "I'll have you know that I'm a beloved local character who has been the award winning gardener at the Hall, man and boy."

His sister sneered, "Well I wasn't impressed by the boy and I can't see the man, so how much of the rest is true?"

Looking around the table, she raised a finger "Beloved?" she asked.

A silence filled the room which she accepted as, 'No comment.'

A second finger was raised, "Award-winning?" she asked

"Prize twerp," muttered Ronald.

Pippa raised two more fingers saying, "Local and Hall puzzle me."

Ronald was enjoying this, so he supplied, "He lived in a shed behind the Hall before it burnt down."

"The shed?" asked Pippa curiously.

"No, the Hall" sniggered Ronald "You would have thought that his leeks would have doused the flames wouldn't you?"

The Commissioner smiled in spite of herself, "It's not often I meet a fugitive from justice with such a sense of humour Ronald, and your wanted poster doesn't do you justice."

Ronald looked around to see if the joke was shared but everyone was avoiding his eye, so he sat quietly from then on as the Commissioner allowed her eyes to roam.

"Margery is it?" she asked next and Margery tensed slightly before nodding.

"Ms Plumm smiled. "I really admire anyone who is capable of keeping a family together, especially unruly boys."

Margery relaxed as she replied, "Oh, I only have two and they went into good jobs after university, but we keep in touch."

The Commissioner raised an eyebrow and Margery sensed a trap.

Ms Plumm paused before saying, "But I meant the mafia dear." With a last sneer at Percy, the Commissioner left them to it and drove The Chief Inspector and Hannah Cuffs back to their headquarters.

The occupants of the kitchen had just relaxed when the three constables entered and glared at Cuthbert.

The left-hand constable hissed, "I've got my eye on you."

The centre-constable added, "So have I."

The right-hand constable joined in with, "Me too."

Henry couldn't resist this one and he seemed to be the only one with nothing to fear, so he joined in with, "It's a good job you don't need spectacles then lads."

All three constables turned towards him and asked "Why?"

"Well, have you ever seen a pair of spectacles with three lenses?"

They all glared at him in communal silence, so Henry sighed and explained. "All three of you are keeping an eye on Cuthbert, so either you would all need a monocle each or a set of glasses with three lenses."

Henry sat back, pleased with his humorous riposte.

After a pause, the three constables stared at Henry and broke the silence.

The left-hand constable said, "I've got my eye on you."

The centre constable added "Me too."

The right-hand constable narrowed one eye and said, "Me too."

Henry looked from one to the other and muttered, "Oh good grief."

* * *

The new mafia control room looked like something from a science-fiction film, one of those where everyone pretended to hang on to something when they were pretending that the pretend space-ship had been hit by a pretend proton torpedo.

Jasper was pleased and his men were impressed, when all these TV's came on they could catch up on the latest cowboy films.

The roofers had packed up and left without many of the tools they had come with and the electricians were trying to account for all the cable they had apparently used.

The plasterers seemed to be fine because the mafia hadn't figured out a use for big bags of powder and anyway, they took their tools home with them.

The painters had started at the end where the plaster was dry and they were constantly puzzled by the number of tins which were actually empty when they prized the lids off.

The DIY craze in the next valley was now resulting in everyone's living room looking like the interior of one of Her Majesty's prisons.

A few days later when the painters had finished, the furniture began to arrive and disappear only to be reordered again.

So far the water-cooler had been safe because the mafia used it to wash 'forensics' off their hands when they left, but the new photo-copier had been swapped for Mrs Biggle's old one.

A few days later Commissioner Plumm and Chief Inspector Peebles Gathered in the control room with WPC Hannah Cuffs and selected members of the community who just happened to be the same members who raised the most suspicion amongst the constabulary.

The Commissioner read a short speech which promised the locals that this new state of the art police station would make the Valley a safer place and ensure that their belongings did not go astray.

The locals could not resist glancing around and spotting gaps where furniture and fittings should have been.

The Commissioner then paused for dramatic effect and turning to the head electrician said "Right, let's make it happen."

The man threw a switch on the huge fuse-box and watched proudly as absolutely nothing happened.

Commissioner Plumm looked slowly back at the electrician as if her authority could solve the problem with the force of her personality and the man began desperately flicking the switch off and on with a maniacal grin on his face.

The screens stayed stubbornly opaque and Henry could stand it no longer, "Didn't anyone tell you that there is no electricity in the Valley?" he asked innocently.

Eyes darted everywhere as people calculated the chain of command and the correct percentage of blame to allocate, but gradually all eyes settled upon the hapless electrician.

"That's ridiculous," he spluttered "Why would anyone ask us to build a state of the art police station where there was no electricity."

"Didn't you check?" snarled the Commissioner.

"Do you check if the cells are there before you arrest anyone?" he snapped back in desperation.

"Not necessarily, as I may have to prove any minute now" breathed Ms Plumm.

The three constables snapped to attention, "Leave it to us Ma'am" they said in unison and clumped down the stairs together.

Everyone waited expectantly with the Commissioner silently daring anyone to meet her eye, but Percy noticed that she was avoiding the spot where he was standing and he smiled.

The three constables returned.

The left-hand constable said. "They're lying Ma'am."

The centre-constable added. "It's not true Ma'am."

The right-hand constable finished with. "All lies Ma'am."

Commissioner Plumm scanned the bewildered faces of the locals and faced the three constables. "Why are they lying?" before snapping "*Just one of you.*"

The left-hand constable jumped forward quickly and said "There is electricity in the Valley Ma'am, we proved it."

The centre constable couldn't restrain himself "We switched them on Ma'am, they all worked."

The Commissioner gave a resigned sigh and nodded to the right-hand constable who seemed about to explode, "All the blue flashing lights on the cars work Ma'am."

Commissioner Plumm lowered her head and slowly left the room to seek out her office and if the mafia had left her a chair, she might just sit and have a good cry.

Henry approached the three Constables and gently pointed out that "The blue-lights are powered from batteries in the cars, boys." Then he patted each one on the shoulder and left.

The police station stood alone and empty like a monument to the folly of bringing officialdom to the Valley, the wind whistled eerily through the radio mast and the surrounding hills looked on smugly.

In her own office back where everything worked and a switch actually caused something to happen, Commissioner Plumm was trying to convince her superiors that there really was a place where coffee machines and computers didn't work and she needed extra funding for generators now and a mafia-proof building to put them in.

Apparently there had been several generators at the site of the cinema built by someone called Aunt Liza (shudder), but she had taken one set with her when she left, the mafia had sold another set to a travelling circus company after its stay in the Valley and another set had been destroyed whilst powering spotlights for the inauguration of the council's Monument to the Fallen when the memorial slabs had been undermined by a radioactive substance which melted the top of the hill.

Glancing up from her notes, Pippa Plumm noted the slack-jawed faces staring back at her and suddenly realised why she was having such trouble getting all the materials she needed. "We're doing wonders for the crime figures already" she added desperately, whilst sliding the requests for replacement furniture under her notes.

Chapter Thirty-Four

In the bar of The Mandrake Arms, Margery listened fondly as Mrs Biggle, Elspeth, Geraldine and Avril chatted about various ailments. It soon became a competition to see whose joints hurt the most or whose kidneys, heart and lungs were failing.

Margery referred to it as their 'organ recital'.

* * *

In Cuthbert's kitchen, the men were doing something they had never expected to have to do; they were trying to make Percy talk.

He didn't respond to any questions about his sister or immediate family at all, even when Ronald mischievously suggested marrying Pippa and becoming his brother-in-law.

Of course with Pippa being in the police force, she was already 'in law' and the Captain pointed out that another girl in the family may become a sister-in-law and it would be utter confusion when the in-laws came to visit.

Ronald pointed out that Percy would of course be the 'outlaw.'

This kept them all busy and no-one heard the panel close quietly as Percy slipped away.

* * *

Jasper had convened a meeting to explain to the mafia why the profits were down this week.

Quite simply, it was because the new basement wall had blocked the disguised tarpaulin and they were having to carry furniture up the stairs and through all the workmen instead of straight into the tunnels and even the workmen didn't accept that they were delivery men because they were going in the wrong direction for a start.

Jasper had been trying to ignore someone jumping up and down at the back with his hand in the air for a while now, but with a sigh he snapped, "Cecil, if you need to be excused, just go."

But Cecil simply came to the front quivering like a hunting dog waiting for the off, so Jasper gave in and waved him to say his piece.

"Well," began Cecil with a sly sideways glance at Jasper "I anticipated this and so I offered to help the bricklayers when they did that particular wall."

"We thought you were just getting out of the heavy lifting" Jasper sneered.

Cecil continued even though faced by yawns and rolling eyes from his audience, "By the time we reached the bit opposite the tarpaulin, the brickies trusted me to smooth the mortar joints on the inside so that they could move on faster, so, whilst the mortar was still wet I started slipping thin pieces of wood into the joints, this pushed the mortar out of the other side where no-one was checking and then I smoothed the joint to hide the wood."

He paused to note that the yawns had stopped, the eyes had stopped rolling and were all fixed on him and even Jasper's sarcasm had dried up. "After that," he continued "I went round the other side, lifted the tarpaulin and scraped all the mortar off so that it wouldn't stick. We should be able to make an opening easily now and carry on with taking stuff through the tunnels."

The mafia broke into spontaneous applause and they all gathered around Cecil congratulating him.

Jasper had to shout to make himself heard when he asked, "And how do we disguise this hole after we use it then genius?"

Cecil waved the problem away with, "The brickies had big square boards with samples of all the brick facings on them, so I borrowed one to fill the hole, no-one will notice."

Jasper gaped as the adulation washed over Cecil. Perhaps it's time to send this one on a training course abroad, he thought.

* * *

Inside the tunnel, the tarpaulin was lifted and they took turns taking karate kicks at the wall, which soon collapsed. The debris was hidden in the tunnel and the fake brick wall was soon in place.

Jasper was pretty much relegated to onlooker status as all the back-slapping passed him by.

As Cecil walked past Jasper after proving his theory, he whispered, "Second in command, I would have thought eh, Jasper?"

Jasper nodded dumbly.

Chapter Thirty-Five

The bricklayers were back the next day and they seemed surprised to see the original building still there, but they started laying more foundations for the generator house.

No-one was sure whether they had made a profit on this job or not because until the book-keepers had assessed how much material had been used or gone missing, the only thing they could be sure of was that they would certainly remember this job, and mostly so that they would remember to never visit this Valley again.

* * *

Percy had been missing all day and he had watched carefully from inside the tunnels as the mafia had found a way into the basement. This was of great interest to Percy, because this was where the cells were and he liked to adjust his potential second home to his liking before he actually took up residence.

As soon as everyone had gone, he removed the wall panel and entered the cell area. This was perfect, none of the alarms or cameras was working and apparently the cell-door locks were electric.

Percy pulled a combination tool from the depths of his welly and started work on the wiring. He began to whistle an unknown aria from a long-lost opera which only he was privy too, in other words he made it up as he went along.

* * *

At last, the time came for a second grand opening and everyone assembled in the control room.

An electrician stood guard at the generator room and another one threw the switch. All the closed circuit television screens flickered into life and the High Street could be seen from all angles at the same time.

The pot plant in the corner shivered slightly. Without the tunnels, the adults would have been in charge now, all right.

Everyone in the control room applauded politely and made to leave as there didn't seem to be any snacks laid on, but the three constables were blocking the door.

Commissioner Plumm eased her notebook out from a perfectly tailored pocket and flipped it open. Her smile was almost beatific as she announced, "Now that the cells are in action and the crime rates need to be under control, I have the authority to detain certain members from the local community to ensure that it stays that way.

The outer doors are all locked and they will not be released until the following people are in custody. So, if the following criminals will accompany me to the cells."

The villagers in the room looked at each other and Cuthbert wondered if that's where the snacks were, so he prepared to follow.

"Percy Plumm," read out his sister with relish.

"Ronald Chisolm" she added.

"Jasper," she said, before adding "And leave the pot plant where it is."

There was a pause before the Commissioner added almost reluctantly, "Margery."

Amidst the gasps of astonishment, the accused began to head downstairs where they stood bemused in the cells which had solid side walls and barred doors to the front.

At a hand signal to the CCTV camera, the cell doors slid shut and Ronald, Margery, Jasper and Percy were left in their new homes.

Margery hissed through the bars to Jasper and Ronald, "I hope you two have a cunning plan to get us out of this mess."

The silence confirmed her worst fears.

Chapter Thirty-Six

Back at the Mandrake Arms the reality was beginning to dawn, Henry was staring into space and the Captain poured him a pint and with an attempt at cheering him up said, "Come on old chap, simply phone your solicitor and get him to sort it out."

Henry sighed, we don't have a solicitor; we usually call the mafia."

The Captain perked up immediately and crossed the room to converse with the pot plant in the corner.

After watching his friend shaking all its leaves and kicking the pot, Henry reminded him that Jasper was in a cell next to Margery.

After a moment's silence the Captain tried to draw another pint, only to be met with a gurgling noise. "Hmm," mused the Captain "Who's going to put a new barrel on?"

Henry slumped even further, "Why do you think I'm depressed?" he asked mournfully.

* * *

Commissioner Plumm and WPC Hannah Cuffs descended the stairs to the cells because there was no lift.

It may be a state of the art police station, but the stairs were traditional.

Many a set of trial notes contained the question, "Why does the accused have two black eyes officer?" followed by the reply "He became unruly Ma'am and fell down the stairs."

It just wouldn't do to tamper with tradition.

The Commissioner started at the end where Percy sat forlornly on his bench looking up like a deprived Panda waiting for his bamboo shoots.

"And how are you this morning Mister Plumm?" she asked brightly, receiving a grunt which further confirmed the Panda analogy.

"Not feeling chatty eh?" she continued "That must be a first for you, brother."

Moving on to the next cell, she found Ronald staring at a spot on the wall in preparation for his interrogation.

Ms Plumm giggled, "Oh you army types, that technique never works you know, because we sit you in front of a different wall."

Whatever Ronald's reply was, it was drowned out by a shriek from Hannah Cuffs outside Margery's cell at the other end of the row.

It sounded oddly like, "Oh I do like your curtains, and they match the throws too."

The Commissioner left Ronald and dashed past Jasper until she stood looking into Margery's domain.

There were curtains, and throws and chrome shelves full of cosmetics, it was better than *her* hotel room.

WPC Hannah Cuffs rightly interpreted all the spluttering and gesticulating as an instruction to go and check the CCTV footage, so she dashed back upstairs.

Pippa Plumm slowly walked back down the row of cells. Somehow, she had missed the fact that Ronald was wearing overalls full of pockets that he hadn't been wearing when he came in and there was a pile of chocolate wrappers under Jasper's bunk.

Percy however was just as despondent as when she had ever seen him.

There was something very odd here and she returned to the control room to check the camera footage for herself.

As soon as she was out of earshot the sniping began.

Margery began it quite reasonably with "Lovely lad that Cecil, I feel quite at home here you know and if the food is bad, he's promised to have some sent in."

Jasper retorted with, "He's an upstart; he's been picking my brains for ages."

Ronald snarled, "Well I wish he'd picked someone else's then, he might have brought the tactical overalls with stuff in the pockets."

Percy never said a word, he had a distinct feeling that when the mafia had come to rescue them and he had shouted "Leave this to me everybody" and touched the two wires together on his door fusing the whole row of doors together that everyone somehow thought it was his fault.

The duty officer in the mafia's headquarters had been absolutely fascinated, the team had gone in but instead of bringing everyone out they ended up taking stuff in and for some reason they had forgotten to leave Percy a ration pack.

The CCTV cameras showed nothing untoward and the whole thing was a mystery, the only bonus was that no-one had escaped from this hugely expensive outpost of law and order, otherwise Pippa Plumm may have found herself back on duty trying to stop Royal Princes wandering off when they heard an Ice-Cream van.

* * *

Cecil was beginning to see that there was more to leadership than he thought, everyone was staring at him and expecting him to solve things, even though it had been that clot Percy who had welded all the doors together. He adopted a confident pose and began wracking his brains for an answer.

* * *

The novelty of Margery's confinement was wearing off now and hearing Ronald and Jasper arguing over what the best method of escape would be, if only they had brains and equipment was becoming too much for her.

With a sigh, she took out a hair-grip and let her hair tumble onto her shoulders; she then straightened the metal grip and set to work on the lock, she was right. Because, she was further along the block, Percy's incompetence hadn't reached this far.

Ronald and Jasper were passing pieces of toilet paper through the bars to each other with elaborate plans drawn on them, when Margery casually sprayed hairspray on the camera lens and walked past them both, removed the wall panel and stepped through the hole.

As they gaped, the wall panel was replaced from the other side and she was gone.

Commissioner Plumm and WPC Hannah Cuffs stormed back down the stairs and gaped uncomprehendingly at Margery's empty cell.

They had been upstairs looking at the screens only minutes ago. Admittedly, the picture was slightly fuzzy, but they should have seen something. Pippa approached Jaspers cell and smiled at him, "Well," she said "That's a mystery isn't it?

Margery seems to have walked through the wall."

To her astonishment, Jasper started to shake and seemed on the verge of tears. "She does that," he whispered.

"Does what?" asked Pippa, hoping she had misheard.

Jasper looked around furtively and the Commissioner instinctively came closer to the bars to hear him. "She runs the coven, why do you think we do everything we're told?"

Ronald barked, "Be quiet Jasper, you'll be the death of the pair of us."

Pippa walked to Ronald's cell, but he was hunched over on his bench as if he daren't move and he was deathly pale.

Also, checking on Percy, she noticed that he was still silent and withdrawn, he didn't even look up.

Returning to Jasper, the Commissioner asked how long this had been going on and Jasper sobbed that it was all he could remember, it was as if he had been under some sort of spell until the police came and now he could see clearly for the first time.

Pippa had certainly heard of these rural communities who thrived on witchcraft to control the locals and there was always a promotion following high profile cases like that.

Turning to the cells she asked, "If I released you boys would you be my eyes and ears until I have all the evidence I need?"

Ronald and Jasper nodded enthusiastically and an electrician was called to sort out the glitch in the new electric doors.

Just as they were about to ascend the stairs, Ronald put his hand in his pocket and went back to Percy's cell, "There you are mate, don't say we don't care" and he pushed a fresh bamboo shoot through the bars as Percy glowered at him.

* * *

Meanwhile, Margery was putting her own plan into action and there were signs outside The Mandrake Arms offering free pies. It wasn't long before they heard a screech of brakes and the door darkened.

"Why, Constable Beeching, do come in" invited Margery with a voice designed to lure sailors onto the rocks.

Beeching was on his third pie when he noticed that the room was filling up. He nodded to Henry and the Captain and then to Ronald who entered with Elspeth shortly afterwards.

Jasper took up his place behind the pot plant and Margery sat down opposite the constable.

* * *

Percy had never felt so alone, he sat there morose and trying to figure out if there was some clever code behind giving him a bamboo shoot, but in the end he just sighed and nodded off.

He woke up again as a scraping noise disturbed him and he watched as the wall panel was removed and a mysterious figure entered and began to pass his cell.

"About time," said Percy just before Mrs Biggle covered him in powder before continuing on her way.

The next one through was Cuthbert who came straight to the bars and demanded to know why Percy was late for dinner, they would be having sliced gravy again.

Percy threw his hat on the floor, jumped on it and quickly made up for all the time he had been quiet.

Cuthbert waited for the storm to calm and then slowly opened the door to Percy's cell. Percy went quiet.

"Didn't it occur to you that when the other doors were released, yours would be too?" asked Cuthbert and they argued their way down the tunnels forgetting all about Mrs Biggle and her strange mission.

* * *

As Margery gazed at Constable Beeching, the mafia formed a circle around them with Jasper standing at the officer's side. He slid a cut-throat razor from his pocket and flipped the blade open, twisting it to catch the light.

At first, the constable thought that Jasper was offering to cut his pie up for him, but the atmosphere was making his senses tingle as he tried to remember all he had learnt on that one day detective course. 'Set everyone at their ease' sprang to mind, followed by 'try not to sound too official.'

133

"Lovely pie, this Margery" he began, with followed by "Careful with that blade sonny, we don't want any accidents now do we?"

Margery smiled, "Oh it won't be an accident constable; we promise you that."

The sweat began to run down Beeching's back as he wondered what had been put in the pies, still, he had to admit that it was a tasty way to go and he reached for another piece.

Margery sensed him drifting, so she nodded to Jasper who neatly sliced one of the officer's shiny tunic buttons off.

Constable nearly dropped his pie, but his self-discipline was very impressive "Here, that's an official Police shiny button that is," he yelped.

Margery leaned forward, "Now pay attention PC plodhopper, it's your fault that we have this damned woman interfering in our lives, you brought her in, you get her out."

Constable Beeching blew out his cheeks, "Well I don't know about..." he began, but the razor moved with a slight whisper and another shiny button clattered across the floor.

The conversation went on like this, until Beeching had lost all his buttons and epaulets and he only had his collar numbers left.

It was horrifying for him. Without the shiny bits, his uniform may as well have belonged to a bus conductor and if they cut his numbers off, he wouldn't even know who he was.

Constable Beeching collapsed sobbing and it was only partly because the mafia had finished the pies. He was putty in their hands and Jasper put his razor away and went to see why Cecil was frantically waving to him at the door.

Mrs Biggle finished her task and stood admiring all the television screens in front of her, she shook her head. It was no wonder they never responded to her calls with all this lot distracting them. She took out her powder compact to test it and see which screen would light up when she rang them, she sighed as they all disappeared in a cloud of scented dust.

Chapter Thirty-Seven

The generator house had been the last straw for the accounts department, there had been no mention of it on the estimates and as for the length of cable used in the job, they could have lassoed the sun and brought it closer, so they could all holiday at home.

Accountants had a natural allergy to empty columns on their books, but columns overflowing weren't well received either. They would need answers and they would need them soon.

This reminded one of the older members from accounting of a police officer who had been sent abroad to liaise with a foreign force and he had sent in a claims form for several hundred pounds. When this was queried, the officer stated that it was for buying a camel as patrol cars were in short supply. This excuse was not accepted and the office drafted a telegram demanding that he bring the camel home with him as they apparently owned it.

A week went by before the officer sent in another claim for the camel's funeral expenses; they were still not convinced that a headstone had been necessary.

* * *

Two of the gentlemen from this very office now sat opposite Police Commissioner Plumm and she watched as their eyes roamed the room mentally matching the furniture to the claims she had submitted.

They had gone through the costing of the building work and commented that it almost cost as much as the Taj Mahal, but they did reluctantly accept that the white marble wonder of the world had been built some time ago.

The knock on her door was a welcome interruption, even if she did recognise the bulk of PC Beeching behind it. The constable entered sheepishly and apologised for interrupting her interrogation of two obvious criminal types.

The accountants narrowed their eyes and began flicking through pages of notes. The name Beeching rang a bell somewhere, they thought.

Constable Beeching wobbled into something like a respectful stance in front of the desk and it gave the Commissioner time to realise that he didn't look like a constable at all; he looked like a giant black hole.

"Where are your buttons? You're out of uniform," she snapped at him (Suppressing a shudder at the thought of seeing Beeching out of his uniform) and watched in amazement as he produced them from his pocket and laid them in a neat row across her desk.

"I've court-martialled myself and written a report listing all the false claims I made," he said, producing a scrunched up piece of paper.

He then held his hands in front of himself, but after trying to reach around his own stomach there was still a gap that could not be spanned by any handcuffs the police force had ever owned.

She waved him away and he left silently.

Commissioner Pippa Plumm felt her doomed career settle across her shoulders like dust from Cuthbert's roof when Percy slammed the door.

One of the accountants studied her carefully as he asked, "So, none of this expense was necessary in the first place then Commissioner?"

Pippa Plumm added this question to the one her superior had asked her last night, "Does this enthusiasm for establishing a remote outpost of the law have anything to do with a vendetta against your brother, Commissioner?"

She sighed; it seemed that at a certain point in a woman's career the questions kept coming, but the answers were just out of reach. Maybe, that was what the glass ceiling did.

She followed the accountants out to their car and made sure that the three constables formed an honour guard and WPC Hannah Cuffs and the Chief Inspector were present.

* * *

Ex-constable Beeching had joined the crowd outside the Mandrake Arms and they watched as all the officers shook hands with each other, the air of finality was unmistakeable. Of course, at moments like that when everyone concentrates upon one spot, the likes of the mafia and even Geraldine automatically make their move.

The mafia encircled Mrs Biggle with the intention of asking why their explosive stores were low and covered in peach-blossom powder and at the same time as Geraldine decided to have one last shot at Cuthbert.

Percy was determined to see his sister leave, so he pushed into the crowd causing Cuthbert to stumble sideways and of course with Percy being shorter than his friend, the dart hummed over his head and struck Cecil who fell against Mrs Biggle causing her to press a button in her pocket.

Mouths gaped, as the middle two floors of the new police station exploded outwards causing the roof to drop perfectly into place to make it a one storey building.

The accountants were seen whispering urgently to Police Commissioner, Pippa Plumm and her shoulders sagged as she got into the back of their car and it drove away.

The rest of the force followed suit with the three constables jammed into the back of a car with the windows down shouting, "Neh-nah-neh-nah," because the mafia had stolen their siren and a silent escort just didn't seem right.

The crowd now gathered around Mrs Biggle and Margery asked, "How on earth did you learn to do that dear?"

Mrs Biggle shrugged before replying, "Mr Biggle was a property developer just when bungalows became fashionable and people wanted to downsize, so he pioneered that method of converting houses to bungalows while people were out shopping. He undercut everyone else because it took the other builders, weeks."

Henry chimed in with "And the village has electricity now, oh!"

The generator house disappeared, before the sound reached them.

"That was our new club house," wailed Jasper.

"That was our power supply," hissed Henry.

"That was the last of the explosives," pointed out Mrs Biggle. "We didn't want these young lads getting their hands on it now, did we?"

Margery looked at Mrs Biggle and sighed, "Why didn't you leave it as it was and have a stair-lift dear?"

Mrs Biggle smiled wryly as she replied, "Oh they don't go fast enough Margery. I need to get there before I've forgotten why I went up."

"Plus," added Henry with a frown; "We no longer have a power supply for it anyway."

Jasper looked down at Cecil, well at least he should be asleep long enough for Jasper to be re-elected and someone under his spell appointed as second in command.

PC Beeching rightly assumed that his scrunched up piece of paper covered in misdemeanours had been destroyed and he was last see trying to bend down to retrieve his buttons which had been distributed far and wide by the explosion.

His brow furrowed as he concentrated on the message squawking at him through his radio. Apparently, a van full of envelopes for the new post office had crashed into a car and with Avril listening in behind him the headline began to write itself "Stationery van crashes into stationary car."

Mrs Biggle simply assumed squatter's rights and moved into her new post office, the mafia sold the radio mast for scrap and brought her some cheap fittings and even found her a metal grill to separate her from the customers.

Her first customer was Cuthbert holding a bunch of flowers he had picked for her on the way over and she glared suspiciously through the grill, "Have you pushed to the front again Cuthbert?" I've got my eye on you."

Cuthbert smiled. 'The world had tilted back again to where it belonged,' he thought.

~ The End ~

138

About the Author

Patrick Barrett is a sixty year old ex-miner from Mansfield in Nottinghamshire. He is married to Paula and between them, they have several children. 'Shakespeare's Cuthbert' was his first book, though he has been writing comedy for several years.

His aims as a writer are 'to be successful and make people laugh by providing them with an escape from the harshness of real life'.

His other abiding interest is in antiques.